'A hug[illegible] teenage girlhood. Menacing, heartfelt and often very funny, Natasha Devon is a new YA voice to watch.'
Juno Dawson

'A sensitive yet powerful portrayal of what it is like to live with anxiety.'
Poorna Bell

'Brilliant on female friendship and the humiliation and confusion when it turns poisonous. Will give a lot of readers greater confidence to identify toxic relationships.'
Mhairi McFarlane

'A deeply compelling and beautifully written story with characters you can't help but fall in love with. Through the eyes of her mixed-heritage protagonist, Natasha perfectly captures the conflict of identity and belonging that many people will be able to relate to.'
Natalie Morris (author of *Mixed/Other*)

'An insightful testament to the fact that the most important relationship we'll ever have is the one with ourselves.'
Anna Williamson

'*Toxic* is simply unputdownable – from the first encounter with its characters to the flawless intersection of plots and twists that navigate the grey shades of feminism, race and privilege – Natasha Devon doesn't hold back.'
Dr Shola Mos-Shogbamimu

Also by Natasha Devon

More praise for *Toxic*

'I wish I could travel back in time and give this book to my teenage self.' ***Coco Cole***

'I wish Natasha Devon had been writing books when I was a teenager!' ***Bryony Gordon***

'Natasha is the cool older sister all teens need in their lives. She truly cares about the mental wellbeing of young people and this makes her such an exciting new author of YA fiction.'
Holly Bourne

'Timely, thought-provoking and totally moreish.'
Chris Russell

'Young adult fiction at its finest.'
Netgalley review

'I would recommend this to anyone who enjoys a good read and especially those who have teenage daughters.'
Netgalley review

'This was one of those books I just couldn't stop reading. I devoured it in two days, even reading until 5 a.m. because I just had to finish it.'
Netgalley review

'The writing is superb and enthralling.'
Netgalley review

BABUSHKA

NATASHA DEVON

uclanpublishing

This is a work of fiction. All the names, characters, businesses, places, events and incidents in this book are either a product of the author's imagination or used in a fictitious manner. Any resemblance to actual persons, living or dead, or actual events is purely coincidental.

Babushka is a uclanpublishing book

First Published in Great Britain in 2023 by uclanpublishing
University of Central Lancashire
Preston, PR1 2HE, UK

978-1-915235-63-3

1 3 5 7 9 10 8 6 4 2

Set in 10/16pt Kingfisher by Amy Cooper.

A CIP catalogue record for this book is available from the British Library.

Printed and bound in Great Britain by Clays Ltd, Elcograf S.p.A.

To my lovely nan, Sylvia. Thank you for all the love and care, gifting me a life-long love of Tom Jones and (inexplicably) ironing my knickers. Thank you also for showing me how to stand up for what I believe in and teaching me never to buy anything from the front of the shelf in the supermarket.

PROLOGUE
June 2001

I have a fear of looking into telescopes.

It's really embarrassing and anyone I've tried to talk to about it has taken the piss. To be honest, even I don't totally understand why. I only know that every time I try to put my eye to a telescope, I instantly get an unpleasant fizzy sensation in my stomach and my limbs turn to jelly.

I got that same feeling just before the moment that changed everything. I didn't have the strength to hold myself up. I kind of folded in on myself, like one of those weird collapsing plastic donkeys you can buy at the seaside. I forgot how to breathe. Everything felt as though it was happening in slow motion.

Later, I wondered whether the thing that actually scares me is reality. When you look into a telescope, it forces you to think about how massive the universe is. How tiny and insignificant your life and your worries are by comparison. It can't just be me who finds that overwhelming.

Watching the blue lines appear on the plastic stick was similar in a lot of ways. You go your whole life believing you can control what happens. Seventeen years I'd believed that.

Then I was slapped by fate. I felt tiny and helpless and stupid.

I had been so sure that it was all a coincidence. I remembered an article I read once called 'Five Reasons You Have Sore Boobs (And How to Fix Them)'. None of them involved a plastic stick and blue lines. I'd missed a few periods, but so had Carrie Bradshaw in season one. She was worried about nothing, it turned out. Somehow, I thought this would all end up being a meaningless blip in my own *Sex and the City*-inspired fantasy.

But this was reality, where my top cost £9.99 from New Look and I had a mammoth decision in front of me I wasn't ready for. If only I could rewind time. Or even just press pause for a bit. There were too many thoughts whizzing around in my mind and I couldn't focus on any of them.

I sat on the edge of the bath and put my head between my legs, trying desperately to focus. I just had to work out who I could tell about this. Did it have to be someone who knew me? Confessing to anyone I knew would involve coming clean about so many other things.

I could write to an agony aunt, maybe. Use a fake name. Perhaps someone already had. The solution to all of this could be waiting for me in the stack of *Adept* magazines piled in the corner of my room. It was worth a shot, I decided. Anything that might help me deal with this without dropping a bomb on my entire life.

That was when I heard Wyn's keys in the door.

She didn't call out 'hello darling!' as she usually did. I just heard her sigh as she kicked off her shoes and hung her handbag on the hook in the hallway. It occurred to me that she might not know I was home.

I stood, shakily, and looked at myself in the mirror above the sink. I looked like a ghost. My eyes were huge, my skin even paler than usual. I was blurry around the edges, somehow. I wasn't going to be able to hide this from her.

I picked up the stick with its blue lines and turned the door handle. Maybe Wyn would know what to do. Perhaps she wouldn't get angry or say 'I told you so'. I imagined her making us tea and smoking a fag out of the window, telling me everything was going to be fine. Like she used to before I came to live here. She'd been through something similar herself, she'd probably say. She'd sort everything out. She'd reassure me that I wasn't to worry.

I knew Wyn would be in the kitchen, so I took a deep breath and walked the six and a half steps along the softly carpeted corridor to tell her the news. I drew in a big breath, then stopped.

Wyn looked even worse than I did – like a ghost who had seen a ghost. She was slumped at the kitchen table, a bottle of whisky in front of her, alongside a heavy-bottomed tumbler. She was staring with red-rimmed eyes, not seeming to be looking at anything in particular.

Did she know already, somehow? How could she, though? Unless she'd noticed the lack of sanitary towels in the little pedal bin in our bathroom over the past few weeks? But that was ridiculous. Wyn was a lot of things but she wasn't psychic. It must be, I realised with horror, something else.

'Hi,' I said, cautiously, manoeuvring myself so I was directly in her eyeline. 'Are you OK?'

It was a stupid question when she so obviously wasn't, but I couldn't think of anything else to say.

She blinked, then held out her free hand, the one that wasn't clutching the glass of whisky. I took it and sat opposite her, holding my breath.

'Darling,' she whispered, her voice quiet and somehow dry-sounding. It was so different to how she usually spoke.

'I'm afraid I've had some bad news.'

CHAPTER 1
October 2019

I was snapped out of my teenage memories and back to the present by a squeaking sound, which echoed around the gallery as the oligarch's wife moved her left foot. It was 9.15 p.m. and she'd been facing the wall, unmoving, for so long I had seriously considered removing my shoe and throwing it at her to check she hadn't turned to stone. Instead, I opted for a less violent option and let out a small sigh, hoping it would rouse her from her reverie and we could wrap up this sale.

The piece she'd expressed an interest in was one of my favourites in the collection. It was by an up-and-coming British painter, who'd done a series of cryptic, partial self-portraits – their torso reflected in a car window, their elongated shadow on the grass of a park, their hand as seen from their point of view as they looked down at it. Apparently, the artist learnt that mirrors weren't invented until the fourteenth century and became fascinated by the notion of trying to piece together a sense of physical self from the glimpses you might catch as you went about your day. It reminded me of my first ever attempt at art when I was at college. An attempt to carve out an identity from what the world mirrored back at you.

Maybe that's what sparked the memory of that awful night back when I was sixteen. Months before I got pregnant with Loo but connected in my mind, somehow.

The painting that had immediately captured me (and, it would appear, the oligarch's wife) was the artist's tiny, distorted reflection in their mother's eye. It was a special piece, one I could tell was going to appreciate massively in value once the artist inevitably made a name for themselves. Whilst it was annoying the potential buyer was taking so long to make up her mind, at least she seemed to be thinking. Too often, the uber-wealthy swept into my gallery and just bought whatever they saw first, or whichever piece looked gaudiest.

Finally, the oligarch's wife spoke.

'I think . . . I will take it,' she said.

I plastered on a bright smile as she spun round, even though part of me was sad to see that particular painting leave the gallery and in spite of the fact that my feet were killing me. I'd been on them for almost twelve hours.

'Excellent!' I responded. 'If you follow me to the desk over here, we can arrange payment and shipping details.'

'And we must celebrate!' she insisted.

Bugger. It was customary for me to have a glass of champagne with customers after making a sale, but I was kind of hoping she wouldn't know that.

'Of course!' I said, recalibrating my plans for the commute back home to Surrey and wondering if the meagre funds left in my account each month after I'd paid Loo and Hugh's school fees would stretch to a taxi. I didn't know what time Loo was going to get in but I really wanted to be there when she did.

I reached into the mini fridge under the front desk, taking out a bottle of Bollinger and two flutes. I knew instinctively there was no point trying to fob this woman off with the cheaper stuff. I carefully poured a modest measure for each of us and held her glass towards her, watching as she tottered across the shiny wood floor in her vertiginous heels to grab it.

I'd been working with seriously rich folk for so long and yet they never ceased to enchant and repel me in equal measure. This customer bore all the hallmarks. Clothes which were obviously tailored to fit her toned, slender frame exactly. Hair completely devoid of frizz, professionally highlighted to a subtle honey shade. Skin so smooth, polished and wrinkle-free it almost looked wet. But what really set them apart was the total lack of anything apologetic in their behaviour or demeanour. No club was closed to them, no space wasn't theirs to claim, no experience out of reach.

The oligarch's wife – I ran my eyes discretely down my appointment diary to remind myself of her name (Valentina) – knocked back the glass of champagne in one gulp and held her empty flute out for more.

'It's an excellent choice,' I told her, as I reluctantly poured more booze.

'It is a gift. For my daughter.'

'How wonderful.' I smiled, thinking about how supremely unimpressed Loo would be if I tried to dictate what she displayed on her bedroom walls.

'You have children?'

'Yes. Two. Llewella is seventeen and Hugh is fourteen.'

'You don't look old enough to have a seventeen-year-old,' Valentina said, squinting and stepping a little closer to scrutinise my face.

'Ah . . . thank you.' I blushed, not wanting to go into why I wasn't, really. 'I can't believe she is practically an adult.'

'And yet, we mothers never stop worrying.' Valentina sighed, which surprised me. I suppose I'd just assumed she, like most of her class, had packed her kids off to boarding school as soon as possible in order to continue a lifestyle of shopping and globetrotting.

I felt the champagne I'd drunk warm my stomach and something make me say, 'Actually, Loo is out in town tonight. She doesn't usually go out in London but she made a friend recently who is from up East and . . . I'm happy she's having fun and I never wanted to be one of those parents who got in the way of that but . . . I'll be glad when she is home.'

'Valentina regarded me for a moment, as though I was one of the installations.

'This worry you have,' she said finally, 'it is a babushka worry.'

'I'm sorry?'

'My grandmother, she used to have a set of matryoshka dolls – you know, the ones that go inside one another, getting smaller and smaller?'

'I do know them. We used to call them Russian dolls,' I told her, hoping that wasn't offensive in some way.

Valentina nodded. 'Yes, they are called different things. Where my grandmother came from, they would call them babushka dolls. And she would say, as we get older, sometimes it is not us who reacts to something but one of the smaller babushkas that lives inside us.'

I must have looked confused because she leant across the desk to look me in the eye. 'So, say when you are young you have a thing happen to you and it leaves a scar. It makes a little babushka. And then later, when you are older, another thing happens that is the same. And even though you are older now, and the thing doesn't matter any more, the babushka . . . she starts to cry.'

I imagined all the previous versions of myself, nestled inside me. And then, quite suddenly, I knew exactly which babushka was crying. Loo was out in London. At night. For the first time. With her new friend.

My sixteen-year-old self was, I realised, not just crying, but screaming . . .

CHAPTER 2
August 2000

'I have this theory I was swapped at birth.'

'I know, Cerys. You tell me the same thing every time you get drunk,' he replied, swiping the now-warm bottle of cider out of my hand. I thought about how much of the two inches of liquid left in the bottom would be a combination of our saliva. I concluded it was probably most of it and that was both adorable and gross.

'I'm not drunk!'

I almost toppled off the wall we were sitting on. I grabbed at a jagged brick to steady myself. There was a moment of silence, during which we both silently acknowledged that I was in fact drunk, but would never admit it.

'You won't miss all this, then?' he asked, gesturing at the lush green hills stretched out in front of us. The sun was just starting to dip below the skyline.

I knew, logically, that the landscape was beautiful. We got told at school that artists over centuries had been spellbound by the gorgeousness of my homeland in South-West Wales. Poets had written about it. Even in those Tom Jones records Mam loved, he'd go on about the grass being really, really green.

But, hard as I tried to feel something about it, I just couldn't. Except perhaps resentment that it wasn't the twinkling lights of a bustling city.

A little shiver of excitement ran down my spine as I thought about how, in less than a week, I'd be amongst those twinkling lights, pounding busy pavements, full of anticipation for the adventures ahead.

I nudged his foot with the tip of mine. 'I'll miss *you*,' I said.

I squinted so I could focus and take in his broad rugby-player frame, his square jaw, his head of fair curls. For the millionth time, I was struck by how fond of him I was. For the millionth-and-first time, I wondered why that fondness wasn't enough. I nuzzled my nose into the place where his neck met his shoulder so I could inhale the scent of him. He put his arm around me and kissed the top of my head.

I could feel his Adam's apple bobbing up and down as he swallowed several times in a row. *Please don't cry,* I thought. I didn't think I'd be able to bear it if he cried.

'Have you spoken to your mam yet?' he asked, after he'd got a grip of himself.

'Uhm. No. I'll do it now in a minute,' I replied sleepily, still nestled under his arm.

'Maybe sober up first. Do you know what you're going to say to her?'

'However I say it, it isn't going to make her any less of a bitch about it.'

'Cerys! That's your mam, you can't say that about her.'

Guiltily, I looked down at my scuffed, label-less Converse

knock-offs, imagining they were Jimmy Choos.

Since Da and I had arranged for me to spend the next two years living with Auntie Wyn in London, Mam had barely talked to me. That wasn't particularly unusual. Mam and I had nothing in common and some weeks it felt like the only time we ever spoke was to have a row. I'd always done something wrong, according to Mam. My skirt was too short. I'd been out too late. I was being fussy because I wouldn't eat whatever plateful of calorific slop she had put in front of me.

Part of me wondered whether I could just not say anything before I left in three days' time. Da would have filled her in on the plan and I knew she'd spoken to Wyn about it because I'd heard her doing her special 'we are just as sophisticated as you are in That London' voice on the phone. She was probably relieved I was going. Her and Da were still sickeningly in love after god knows how many years of marriage and I always got the impression I was an inconvenience. My existence was an unplanned interruption in their Love Story.

But then I thought about how Mam always used to tuck me in and tell me stories before I went to sleep as a kid. Or how she'd give me a cwtch as I was heading out of the door to school, even after we'd had an argument, because 'you never know when it's the last time you might see someone'. She used to say that to me constantly and it stuck. Nothing could change the fact she was my mother, however hard I found it to believe. I should at least say a proper goodbye.

'Cerys? You with us?' he asked, placing his index finger under my chin and gently tilting my head upwards.

'Mmmm,' I replied drowsily.

After a moment, he spoke. 'Anyway, you'll probably forget all about me after about a week.'

'I won't,' I mumbled. I kept my eyes closed, partly because I was sleepy and partly because I knew, even then, it was a promise I couldn't keep.

'All set then, are you?' asked Da, gesturing at the chaos that was my bedroom. He reached across to turn the volume down on my mini hi-fi, which was currently blaring out 'Genie in a Bottle'. I was grateful. It's kind of embarrassing to hear Christina Aguilera bellowing about wanting to be rubbed the right way when your da's in the room.

He was, I could only assume, being sarcastic. I'd read an article in *Adept* the other month about a 'capsule wardrobe' – a skirt, pair of trousers and a jacket you could rotate with various tops and accessories to create hundreds of different outfits – and had been trying to decide which clothes I'd be taking with me to London on that basis.

I'd abandoned the capsule wardrobe plan after about five minutes. There was no way I could narrow my options that far. Whenever I pictured myself living in London, I was strutting around like Carrie from *Sex and the City*. And I was pretty sure she had more than one pair of trousers on hand to create her looks.

Last time we'd visited Wyn in Ealing, I'd watched people as we drove past them. I tried to work out what the London vibe consisted of. But there was no thread to it at all. I'd seen people who looked like they'd just come from the gym walking alongside business suits and full-on-glam. Some people wore a mixture of all three at the same time.

Here in Wales, you knew where you were with fashion. It was jeans and a nice top for the pub, a dress for clubbing, strappy sandals at all times. (Which meant putting trainers in your bag for the walk from the bus stop, across fields, then home.) Hair: centre parted, blonde and straightened. Make up: smoky eyes and nude lips. Skin: tanned.

If you could pull off that look (and I could) you were cool. Or hot, depending on who was looking at you.

In London, everyone looked different. It was exciting, in a way. People who would be pointed out and laughed at in my little village because their fashion choices were so 'out there' were just casually going about their day. But it also meant I had no idea what to wear to look like I belonged.

I'd decided the solution was actually to empty the contents of my entire chest of drawers and wardrobe out onto my bed and group things into categories. But then I'd got distracted chopping a rosette off the toe of an old pair of shoes and sewing it onto the corner of one of my tops (Bradshaw-style) before deciding it needed glitter and trying to gild the petals with one of my sparkly nail polishes. The result was my room looking even more chaotic than usual. This was, as Mam was always telling me, saying something.

'I am creating my Art College Aesthetic!' I declared. 'You would not understand.'

There was smile at the corners of Da's mouth, which was infuriating. I wished Wyn was here to talk to. She'd get it.

'Well, so long as you're done by tomorrow and ready to go,' he said and ambled towards the door, taking giant strides with his long legs to avoid the clumps of clothing scattered across the carpet. He turned when he got to the threshold.

'And, er, your mam is downstairs having a cuppa when you have a minute. Go down and chat to her, will you?'

'I'll be down now.'

'Will you, though? Look . . .' He sighed, striding back into the room and perching awkwardly on the cluttered bed. 'I know your mam and you don't always see eye-to-eye, but it was a big thing, her agreeing for you to go so far away, and you've never so much as said thank you.'

I bristled. Why should I thank her? It was my opportunity; I'd earnt it. And it wasn't like she enjoyed my company much anyway. As if reading my thoughts, Da went on, 'She loves you, you know.'

'Funny way of showing it, sometimes.'

'Oh, come on now. That's not fair. Who cooks for you every night, whether you're in to eat or not? Who sits up awake worrying about you when you get home late? Who gives you her family allowance every week to spend on all this?' He gestured at the clothes, shoes, CDs and magazines everywhere.

'It feels like all she ever does is have a go at me.'

'Because she cares, cariad.'

'Hmmmm,' was all I could muster in response.

'Go down now and then it's done,' Da said. I could tell he was getting agitated and that was enough. He'd only ever raised his voice to me about three times in my whole life. He didn't need to. I'd rather die than disappoint him.

Reluctantly, I peeled myself off the floor. I brushed down the front of my jeans, headed onto the landing and down the stairs, past all the shelves full of hideous ornaments and bowls of potpourri. I found Mam in the kitchen, scrubbing at something invisible in the corner behind the kettle. I cleared my throat. I knew she heard me but she didn't acknowledge it. Just carried on scrubbing. I sighed. She was obviously going to make this difficult.

'Mam?'

'Yes?' she replied stiffly.

'Can I talk to you a minute?' I slid into one of the chairs around the massive wooden table at one end of the kitchen and started picking at my left sleeve. She turned ever so slightly in my direction and scrubbed a little less forcefully, which I took to mean that she was listening.

'Uhm . . .' I realised I had absolutely no idea what I was going to say. 'Just wanted to say . . . you know. Thank you?' Is that what I wanted to say? I knew I needed to say something, but was 'thank you' it? I racked my brain.

'Oh yes? What for?' Mam asked, which was annoying. I was the one making all the effort here. She could at least meet me halfway.

'For . . . I guess . . . letting me go to stay with Auntie Wyn.'

'It's not like I had much say in it. You would have gone no matter what I said.'

I sighed. 'Don't be like that.'

'Like what? Like not being overjoyed that my only child

couldn't wait to get away from us? That she'd prefer to live in a big, dirty city full of thieves and criminals? I don't know what we ever did to make you like this, Cerys.'

She'd said this before and it always made me feel like a freak. Why *was* I like this? Why did the thought of living in Carmarthenshire for ever make me feel like I couldn't breathe? I couldn't explain it. I just knew I had to get away.

I suddenly felt that familiar sense of being trapped and stood up forcefully, banging my knees on the table as I did. It hurt, and the pain made me even angrier at Mam.

'THIS IS HOW I AM!' I shouted. 'AND I DON'T NEED YOU MAKING ME FEEL LIKE SHIT FOR EXISTING!'

'Stop being melodramatic, Cerys. And don't swear.'

'URGH!' I exclaimed, throwing my hands up in the air. There was no reasoning with her.

As I stomped out of the kitchen, muttering to myself, I collided with Da. He was leaning against the staircase, his pipe halfway to his mouth.

'That could have gone better,' he said.

I slammed the door, put on my Manic Street Preachers CD and played 'If You Tolerate This Your Children Will Be Next' at maximum volume, five times in a row. I wanted to cover up the inevitable sounds of Mam popping off at Da about my 'behaviour' and him calming her down. But I also wanted them to notice my choice of track. There was a reason it was one of my favourite songs. I wasn't going to let my head be kept down by the weight of Mam's shame.

CHAPTER 3

Mam didn't come to the station to see me off. It was just me, Da and Gruffyd our sheepdog (Gruff for short) in the van.

Gruff, who was behind me on the back seat, kept putting his paws on my shoulders trying to lick my cheeks. I'd freshly applied fake tan that morning, so had to wrestle him off. Da thought it was funny, which exasperated me.

'Da! Make him stop!'

'I can't, I'm driving,' was his response, which was patently bollocks. Gruff was so well trained, even the slightest clearing of Da's throat could make him stop whatever he was doing and sit to attention.

'I don't want to turn up in London smelling of dog spit!' I exclaimed.

'There'll be far smellier things for you to contend with, I'm sure,' Da said mildly, not sensing, or perhaps choosing to ignore, my exasperation.

When we arrived at the station, Da heaved my bags onto the platform and stood with me, waiting for the train to arrive.

'Will you be OK with these at the other end?'

'Yes, Da.'

'They're really heavy. What on earth is in them? Bricks?'

'About fourteen pairs of shoes.'

'Ah. Have you got your mobile?'

I patted my pocket and nodded.

'And is it topped up with credit?'

'Yes. Twenty quid.'

'Phone us when you get to Wyn's, OK?'

'If you had a mobile, I could text you.' We both acknowledged the unspoken end of that sentence – 'and avoid the chance of Mam picking up the landline'.

'Ah! New-fangled things' said Da. I rolled my eyes.

Most of the time I didn't mind my parents being so much older than everyone else's. When it came to using any type of technology, though, it was like trying to explain it to Martians. I often got frustrated.

I don't think my parents had particularly wanted children. They were always making puppy-dog eyes at one another, which was a bit nauseating. I got the impression they were far too wrapped up in each other to want a third wheel to their cosy twosome. When I'd 'come along' it had been a 'nice surprise', they told me. I took that as a euphemism – I had not been planned. I had not been welcomed.

When I was born, Mam was thirty-four, which was ancient for a first-time mother back in the eighties. She was a decade older than most of the other parents at my school and she looked and acted even older than that. None of my friends' mams ever seemed to fuss as much as she did. If it was an Olympic sport, she could fuss for Wales. It felt like she was always on my back, always worrying unnecessarily. It was exhausting.

Mam was, without doubt, the stubbornest person I'd ever known. Take now, for instance. I'd bet my (admittedly not massive) life savings that she would be standing by the window, wringing her hands, looking out over the fields while sighing. She'd be worrying about me getting on a train (like I'm not a fully grown sixteen-year-old). But would she come to the station to see me off? No, she would not. Instead, she kissed me on the cheek and said 'goodbye, Cerys' in a weirdly formal way, before wandering off to (probably) clean something that didn't need cleaning. All because I didn't apologise for our fight the other night. But why should I? I hadn't done anything wrong, apart from not wanting to stay in South Wales like her, wearing beige and baking Welsh cakes until I die. Hardly a crime.

The roar of an engine startled me out of my Mam-based stewing and I turned to see Rhys skidding into the station car park on his moped. We'd said our goodbyes the night before, tucked into his little single bed. We looked out through the open window up at the night sky and reminded each other that, no matter where we each were in the world, we'd always be under the same stars. What was he doing here?

Rhys ran up the steps to the platform, taking off his helmet and shaking his hair loose as he went, like he was in an advert for aftershave. Da, ever discrete, pretended to be fascinated by the framed timetable on a nearby wall as Rhys scooped me into his arms and went in for a snog.

'I'm sorry. I know I said I wouldn't, but I needed to see you one last time before you left,' he panted.

It was so sweet, but so claustrophobic all at the same time. I just stared at him for a moment, blinking. I thought about all the girls at school that had fancied him and how, even though some of them practically offered themselves to him on a plate, it was me he had wanted. The way he looked at me, it was like I was a goddess, or Britney Spears or something. So, I'd let myself go along with it every time he talked about how after I'd got London 'out of my system' we'd get a little house in Llangunnor and start a family . . .

Because that's what I *should* want and it would be so much easier if I did. So, I kept saying it out loud, hoping that one day my feelings would match my words.

Yet, as I heard the distant rumble of the train approaching, I felt a powerful urge to shake him off. I wanted to push him away, tell him to stop smothering me all the time.

'I love you,' he said, kissing my ear wetly. 'I'll let you say goodbye to your da now. Just had to have one last look at you.' He stepped away, hands behind his back, watching me like I was on TV.

'I love you too,' I replied, more as a reflex than because I actually meant it. I was feeling a million emotions at once. Mostly, I was irritated to have had these few precious moments of peace with my da interrupted. Da came with me onto the train, hoisting my bags up onto one of the overhead shelves before giving my shoulder a squeeze and dashing out of the carriage when the beeps announced the doors were about to close.

As the train began to move, Rhys, Gruff and Da stood in

a solemn line on the platform. I wondered what they would talk about once I was gone. Me? Rhys had made it clear he didn't want me to go, but he said he understood it was something I had to do. Da had never really voiced an opinion, other than to occasionally remind Mam that it was my life and I had to make my own decisions. But did he secretly think they were my own *mistakes*?

I waved until they became tiny distant specs and the smile I had been holding in place started to hurt my cheeks. A dull ache had been creeping across my chest and up into my throat as they became smaller and smaller.

As soon as they were out of sight, I burst into tears.

CHAPTER 4

I didn't really know why I was crying, but the more I tried to stop myself the more fresh tears spilled down my cheeks. In the end, I just gave into it. There was no one else in the carriage so I thought I might as well wail like a banshee and get it all out.

I hadn't counted on the ticket inspector hearing me, of course.

'Oh, my poor love,' she said, plonking herself on the seat opposite mine and patting me on the shoulder. 'What you crying for?'

Not wishing to be rude (especially to someone with the power to give me a twenty-quid fine if they felt like it) I smiled in a weak, watery sort of way and tried to find some words. At first, all that came out was a series of hiccups.

'GEMMA!' the ticket inspector yelled suddenly, turning her head and leaning into the aisle between the seats. I heard tinkling as the refreshment cart approached and a voice say 'yes, love?'

'Get this poor girl a cup of tea, will you? She seems like she could do with it.'

An awkward silence followed as Gemma poured boiling

water into a cup and, without asking, added milk and two sachets of sugar. I took it gratefully. I could see they were both trying to be kind.

'Bit better?' asked the ticket inspector, once Gemma had rumbled off in search of paying customers and I'd taken a few sips. I nodded. 'Want to tell me what's up?'

'I think I'm just a bit . . . overwhelmed,' I told her. 'I'm going to live with my Auntie Wyn in London while I study fashion . . . well, it's an art and design course, actually, but I want to do fashion after that. And I'm really excited and I've been looking forward to it for ages but . . . it's a big step, you know? To leave home.'

'I see,' said the ticket inspector, smiling and patting my shoulder again as she stood. 'And I bet you'll miss your mother too, won't you? While you're away?'

'Hmmmm,' I replied, bowing my head over the steaming paper cup.

'Well, I think you're being very brave. And good luck to you. You'll be all right now,' she declared, as she opened the door to the next carriage.

It was a statement, not a question.

I reached for my small case of CDs, which I'd taken out of their covers and slid into flimsy plastic pouches for the journey. I flipped through, trying to find an album that would inspire me to be as brave as the ticket inspector seemed to think I was. In the end, I settled on *Now That's What I Call Music! 1999*. Sliding it into my CD Walkman, I selected 'You Don't Know Me' by Armand Van Helden and imagined I was bellowing the lyrics at Mam. It fit my mood, but just got me more riled up.

Wanting to be soothed, I picked up that week's issue of the *Celebrity Clarion*, which I'd bought from the tiny newsagents by the station. When music didn't work, magazines were guaranteed to immerse me in a world of glamour and gossip and make me forget reality. At least for a while.

I flicked to the Scandal section. That's what I needed: photographic evidence of celebrity bad behaviour. It always made me feel better, knowing these beautiful people with glamorous lives had embarrassing slip-ups, relationship dramas and body hang-ups.

The first entry read:

CAT FIGHT CHLOE

Pop starlet Chloe V was snapped looking a little worse for wear last Friday. Here she is emerging from celebrity hot-spot Red Tie Wans in London's fashionable West End. An insider told CC she hit the bottle after feuding with a well-known glamour model over their mutual ex, footballer Trevor Brooks.

'Chloe called the model a slut and threw her glass of champagne in her face,' the insider shared exclusively with us. 'Everyone was staring, totally shocked. Then Chloe went to the bar and just started chugging back shots.'

Later she was seen dancing on the tables before being escorted out by bouncers. Oh dear! We hope your head didn't hurt too much the next day, Chloe!

The photo showed Chloe V in low-slung jeans and a one-shouldered crop top, revealing her toned abs and protruding hip bones. I would have been jealous, except she was slumped forward, as though halfway through stumbling. Her eyes were almost closed and her hair was all over her face. She looked totally wazzcocked. How embarrassing.

Opposite was *Clarion*'s regular feature, the Square of Doom. It was full of pap shots of celebrities, but with a section magnified inside a red square. The captions read:

DARCY CELLULITE SHOCKA!

TESSA'S WEIRD FOOT!

MELANIE FAKE TAN FAIL!

I hunched over, my face just centimetres from the shiny page as I drank in these small details. Aah, that was better.

I leant back in my chair and, before I knew it, I'd drifted to sleep.

Paddington Station was immense. It was a big, glossy glass building where everyone looked like they were doing something important. I'd never been there before. Da had always driven us whenever we'd come to visit Wyn in London. Although that was rare, to be honest. Wyn mostly came to us in Wales for Christmas. We'd have her and my nain to stay, back when Nain was alive.

That was always my favourite time, when we had Wyn at our farmhouse. She'd sweep in wearing one of her kaftan/turban combos and sit in an armchair telling me stories about London. I'd perch cross-legged on the rug at her feet and drink in her stories about this magical place. Where the street lights were always on and you could get food from anywhere in the world at 2 a.m. Where you could see your favourite musician play an intimate gig to twenty people in the cellar of a bar no one knows about. Where you just bumped into famous people on the pavements, all the time. Where your next-door neighbour could be from somewhere cool like Africa or the USA.

The thing is, Wyn was like me once – a normal girl from rural Wales, descended from a long line of farmers. Yet today she was someone who went to the theatre for fun and hung out with authors. She spoke three languages. She went on holiday every year to the South of France with a group of girlfriends. If she could become a sophisticated being, so could I.

The journey from Paddington to Ealing looked easy on the map. But a map couldn't convey how confusing all the signs at the station were, or how many bloody stairs there were everywhere, or how annoyed London commuters get when you don't move fast enough, or look a bit lost.

Wyn had offered to come and meet me off the train at Paddington, but I didn't want her to think I was a simple country person who couldn't cope with the Tube. If I was honest with myself, I regretted that decision. I got lost four times and had to stop and get out the instructions I'd written down, which Wyn had dictated over the phone. A couple of times I'd thought about asking someone, but everyone looked so busy and angry that I chickened out.

I was sweating and breathing heavily as I turned into her road, pulling two wheely suitcases behind me and carrying an overstuffed backpack on my shoulders. I sighed with relief as her familiar front door came into view.

Wyn lived in a ground floor flat next door to a florist on one side and a delicatessen on the other. Her home was one of my favourite places on earth. It was stylish, but somehow comforting too. Her wine-red sitting room contained two large squishy armchairs, one of which was usually occupied by Mooch, her long-haired American Bobtail. The television in the corner only went on for documentaries or other programmes far too heavy and educational to include adverts. There were no ornaments, like Mam had. Just rows and rows of books on shelves interspersed with the odd interesting bit of art on the walls.

She used bold, jewel-like colours in her decorating. The kitchen was rich ochre, her bedroom was bold turquoise, the spare room (or my room, as I suppose it was now) was emerald green. There wasn't even a hint of beige, anywhere. Everything was for her and just as she liked it, with no apologies.

Wyn had lived alone her entire adult life. Mam once told me she thought Wyn might be a lesbian. Wyn laughed when I told her that. 'I'm not, darling. Not that there's anything wrong with being gay. In many ways, I wish I was, actually.'

'What do you mean?' I asked. I couldn't understand why anyone would choose to be that way when it seemed to make life so much harder. Some girls at my school once got food thrown at them for hugging each other in the lunch hall. I don't even think they were lesbians.

'I suffer from the unfortunate affliction of being attracted to men whilst not being able to stand the company of most of them for more than about eight hours,' she replied. I burst out laughing. 'Of course, I have sex, darling,' she continued, without even seeming to consider that it might be weird to say that to me. This was why I loved her. She was more like a big sister than an aunt. 'I've had more than a hundred lovers, I'm sure. Not that one counts such things. But I just send them on their way after I've given them breakfast so I can spend the rest of the day smoking and reading with my cat.'

She showed me there was an alternative way to live. You don't have to get married and have babies, wear shapeless chunky knits and cook stews. You can just say 'fuck it' and do whatever you want.

Mam and Wyn had never really got on. It's amazing how two people who were born within five years of each other, have the same parents and grew up together can be so different. Mam (Delia) is the eldest and she's a cardigan sort of person – traditional. She was the teacher's pet at school, apparently, on account of being so well behaved. Wyn, in contrast, is loud and colourful and, while very clever, prone to naughtiness. A teacher's nightmare, I'd imagine.

My nain told me they used to fight like cat and dog when they were teenagers in the 1960s. They shared a bedroom and Wyn used to play rock and roll LPs at ear-splitting volumes and dance around smoking fags while Mam was trying to study.

You can tell Mam resents how much I adore Wyn. I can't help it, though. The woman's a legend.

I buzzed the intercom and heard Wyn's familiar posh London twang, with only the faintest hint of Welsh, say, 'HELLO DARLING!' before the front door clicked open. By the time I got to the door of her flat it was flung wide and she was standing there, looking glorious in a maroon and gold kaftan, a matching turban and slippers. She held out both hands towards me in anticipation of a cwtch.

After we'd hugged and squealed at each other for a bit, she held me at arm's length and said, 'You know, if you're going to do the make-up thing you really ought to learn how to put it on properly, darling.'

I glanced at the mirror in the hallway and baulked. My foundation was blotchy and I had wobbly lines of mascara running down my cheeks where I'd blubbed on the train.

'Oh, fuck!' I exclaimed, delighted at being able to swear without being told off. 'I cried earlier and then forgot to check it.'

'Oh, my precious darling angel pet lamb from heaven,' Wyn replied, gesturing down the hallway with one arm. 'I shall put the kettle on and have a ciggy and you shall tell me all about it.'

Leaving my bags at the door, I followed her into the kitchen, breathing a sigh of relief as I went. I was home.

CHAPTER 5

We went out for dinner that evening. Wyn knew a 'gorgeous little place' about ten minutes' walk away. No need to dress up, she said, so I put on my jeans and a little hooded velour top.

The night was warm. The air was still and balmy in a way it never was in Llangunnor. There seemed to be a total absence of breeze. I suppose all the buildings got in the way. As we walked, Wyn pointed out areas of interest.

'That's the boutique that my friend Organza owns, darling. I've told you about Organza – she's from LA and her father is a terribly successful movie director. But she fell in love with an English scriptwriter so now she lives here. You should pop in and introduce yourself, tell her you want to be in fashion . . . Oh, and there's the stop for the bus you must take if you ever want to go into town, darling. It'll take you to Broadway station – although of course you can walk there, too, it's not far – and then you can get the Central Line, you know, that's the red one . . . And that Greek bakery there does the most delicious baklava you have ever had. Tell them you're my niece, they know me in there, darling . . .'

On and on she went, while I nodded. I was trying to pretend

that I knew what she meant by 'going into town'. Which town? Wasn't it all London? Or what baklava was. Or that I thought it was completely normal to be called Organza. It seemed like there was something interesting to see every step we took and I was working hard to keep up, to log the information she was giving me. As though there might be an exam at the end of it.

We reached a restaurant with huge windows and seats spilling outside onto the pavement. There were trees lining the seating area with fairy lights strung in them. It was cute and a bit magical. As we stepped up to the door, a man with light brown skin, shiny hair tied up in a bun and enviably long eyelashes rushed out and enveloped Wyn in a hug.

'Hello, my lovely!' he said, with an accent I couldn't place. 'So good to see you!'

'Hello, darling,' Wyn replied, kissing him on both cheeks. 'I've brought my niece, Cerys. You know, the one who is studying fashion. She's staying with me for a while.'

I tried to be casual, standing there with my thumbs hooked into the belt loops of my jeans. I tried to act as though this was the type of thing I did all the time. Like everything I was seeing and feeling wasn't totally alien to me.

'Welcome, welcome!' he gestured us inside and we sat at a rickety wooden table.

'Have a look at the menu, darling,' Wyn instructed. 'I already know what I want. I always have the calamari to start, then the tagine.'

I looked. I didn't know what any of it meant. Luckily there were descriptions under each dish. I liked the sound of

Mujaddara – lentils and rice with crispy onions – but worried I wouldn't be able to say it when the waiter came to take our order. In the end I chose the thing I was sure I could pronounce. 'Chicken wings, please. And . . . errr . . . couscous salad.' I knew about couscous because there was an article in *Adept* once about how it was the new rice. Apparently all the It girls were eating it.

Wyn and I discussed how I was going to get to college in Fulham the following week. She tried to explain the route by tube and, when I started to go a bit cross-eyed with confusion, she promised to go with me on a trial run the next day.

'And how do you feel?' Wyn asked. 'Excited? Nervous? A bit of both?'

I hesitated, not really knowing. I'd been so focused on actually getting to London, I hadn't even thought about the next bit.

'Mainly excited. I think,' I told her and she nodded and smiled like that was the right answer.

As we talked and ate, I watched the other people coming in for their tea. It was 8 p.m. before we even left Wyn's flat, far later than I was used to eating. Mam would usually have dinner on the table at about six. Yet people were strolling in at half eight, not looking like they were about to faint from hunger or anything. They weren't dressed up, either.

In my whole life, I could count the number of times I'd been to a restaurant on my fingers. Every time, it was a big deal.

Rhys had taken me out for dinner twice – once on my birthday and another time because we'd been going out for exactly one year. We'd planned and talked about each outing for weeks beforehand. I'd worn a posh dress and heels and everyone else in the restaurant looked like they were celebrating something special, too. But the people here looked like they'd made a spontaneous decision to walk in off the street.

Is that what Londoners did? Just wandered around and popped in somewhere when they were peckish? The idea was enough to make my head spin.

'You'll have to explore the Kings Road, darling,' Wyn was saying.

'Oh, yeah?' I replied, watching two men kiss each other on the lips and no one else pay any attention at all.

'David Bowie and Marc Bolan used to go skip diving there, before they were famous. That's where they got a lot of their early stage outfits, legend has it.'

'Who's Marc Bolan?' I asked. It was out of my mouth before I could consider whether I sounded stupid, or uncultured.

'Oh, darling.' Wyn shook her head. 'I can see I have much left still to teach you! Lead singer of T. Rex. And the original mod. Although of course he became a pioneer of glam rock, later on.'

I nodded in the way I imagined someone who understood would.

'We'll play some when we get back,' Wyn promised.

When the bill came Wyn snatched it up, but not before I saw that it was almost £50. Fifty quid! Just on dinner! That was how much I'd earn at my Saturday job and it would have to last me the entire week.

As we wandered back to Wyn's, something felt off. Suddenly,

I realised what it was. It should be dark by now. Yet the lights that cast out from the still-open grocery shops, along with the street lamps, meant it was as bright as midday.

Wyn ducked in to one of the convenience stores. There were so many of them and they all seemed to be selling the same things – magazines, sweets, crisps, alcohol, milk, rows and rows of fizzy drinks in cans. How did they make a profit when there was an identical shop just next door?

'Need some milk,' she said. 'And what do you eat for breakfast, darling?'

I thought about what I used to eat in Wales. If I was honest, I was always trying to skip breakfast. I was invariably running late and Mam was always trying to force porridge down me, which I thought tasted like wallpaper paste.

When I was imagining my life in London it was as though I'd drawn the outline of a painting. It was just these passing snapshots. I'd think about Wyn and me drinking tea in her little kitchen and laughing about something. I didn't know what. Or going shopping on Oxford Street with the new friends I was sure I'd make at college. In these fantasies, I was always glossier, better dressed, cooler.

But I hadn't stopped to think about the little things, like learning how the public transport works and what I'd eat for breakfast. Those little details were the shading – the things that would fill in the space between the lines I'd drawn. It seemed important to pick a breakfast food that matched the person I wanted to be, here. The new me. The real me.

'Uhm, toast?' I replied uncertainly.

'Fabulous!' said Wyn, which made me burst out laughing. Toast was probably the least fabulous food on the planet, but it was the only thing my brain could think of in that moment.

Ignoring me, she went on, 'Now, I have a white farmhouse, I think, but do you like that? They do a lovely chleb pszenny here, if you'd rather?'

'Errr. OK. I'll have that . . . chleb . . . stuff,' I said. I watched as Wyn swung the golden oval loaf onto the counter in its clear polythene bag. It cost £3.

This was a totally different world.

CHAPTER 6

Wyn had taken a few days off work to help me get settled. During the daytime we explored London. Just like she promised, she showed me the route I'd be taking every day to get to college. It was a lot less scary than it seemed on the map. Then she asked me what else I wanted to see.

I wanted to ask if we could go to the big Topshop on Oxford Street, which was legendary. They were always talking about it in *Adept*. Apparently, there was an entire floor dedicated to accessories, as well as a basement with an actual DJ mixing on some turntables while you browsed. They made it sound as though it was half-shop, half-club and I couldn't think of anything more brilliant. But I didn't think it was really Wyn's scene, so instead I said I didn't know what I wanted to do. I said she could decide, since she knew the city so well.

So, we went to Camden Market, the cobbled streets were full of stalls selling vintage clothes, knock-off Doc Martins and delicious-smelling food. We visited Oxford Circus, but walked straight past the big Topshop (which was like torture) so Wyn could show me Broadcasting House, where all the BBC radio stations lived.

Wyn also took me to the V&A – the Victoria and Albert Museum – which had become a bit of a tradition whenever I visited. She'd first taken me there when I'd started talking about wanting to study fashion. I remembered how I'd never seen anything like it – the marble and glass everywhere, the ceilings so high it felt like you might as well be outside. There were sculptures on plinths in the vast entrance hall. Way before the glossy mags containing pap shots of celebs, this was how people captured their image so it could last for ever.

Back then, it had made me think. Did you have to stay still for ages while you were sculpted, like when people sat for paintings? Or did the sculptor do it from memory? Did the subjects get any say in how their body was sculpted? Could you ask for your penis to be made bigger, or your bum a perkier shape?

This time, as I'd passed the familiar marble forms, a new question had occurred. I asked Wyn, 'Do you think it would be better or worse to live in a world before cameras were invented, where the only way people would know what you looked like after you died was from looking at a painting?'

'Oooh, that's a fascinating thought, darling,' Wyn had replied and I'd given myself a little high five for being clever. 'I suppose it comes down to whether you believe you have the right to be remembered as you wished you were? Or is it everyone else's right to know you how you actually were?'

We continued walking in silence for a bit, me thinking about what she'd said.

'And,' she continued, 'with a life consisting of so many

millions of seconds, so many facial expressions and poses and moods, who decides which is the "real" you?'

'OK, my brain's hurting a bit now,' I replied. 'Can we go to the gift shop?'

Wyn laughed. 'I see the gift shop is still your favourite part.'

In the evenings, Wyn and I talked about anything and everything. There was nothing that was off limits in conversations with my auntie. I revelled in the unusual experience of not having to watch what I said. We talked about my life back in Wales (boring beyond all sense), whether I thought I'd marry Rhys one day (maybe), what my parents thought of me moving so far away. She told me about her job. The manuscripts she was working on and which ones she was enjoying the most. Which authors she liked and which she thought were 'pretentious arseholes'.

'Tell me some fashion things you're immersed in at the moment, darling,' Wyn commanded one evening as we sat in the armchairs in her sitting room.

Mooch purred in her lap and there was a few centimetres of red wine in a huge glass on the side table next to her. The soft murmurs of a radio documentary drifted down the corridor from where it was playing in the kitchen.

'Well, according to Veronica Bailey, who is my favourite writer at *Adept*, this season it is all about tactile fabrics,' I replied, parroting a line from Veronica's column.

'Such as?' Wyn asked, taking a sip of her wine. The liquid seemed to take an eternity to reach the rim of the glass and touch her lips. She even drank in an elegant way.

How long did it take to train herself to be like that? I wondered.

'The example they gave was fur. Faux fur, obviously. Apparently, it makes men want to touch you.'

'Oh, for heaven's sake!' Wyn exclaimed crossly. 'So that's why we dress ourselves now, is it? In order to invite men to touch us?'

'Maybe I'm not explaining it right,' I said, getting up and darting into my room to find the latest issue. 'Let me find you what she actually said,' I called out as I searched. 'It's a really good article . . . Here we are,' I said, coming back into the sitting room and placing the magazine in Wyn's lap, open at the article. I sat on the edge of the armchair opposite and watched her read. I was excited for the moment she finished and admitted Veronica is a genius of our times.

WANNA KNOW IF HE LOVES YOU SO?

(It's in his . . . err . . . touch, apparently.)

Veronica Bailey

Think of a woman men find sexy. Chances are, Britney Spears or perhaps Angelina Jolie springs to mind. When we imagine sexiness, we think of how a woman looks. We envisage Britney's enviable abs or Jolie's plump pout.

But what about us mere mortals, those who weren't

born with goddess-like facial features or don't have the time to do the reported one thousand sit-ups per day Spears uses to maintain her washboard stomach? Well, the good news is that new research has shown sex appeal has as much to do with what we feel as what meets the eye.

I don't mean 'feeling confident' (although that's obviously attractive too). I literally mean what you feel like. To other people. Specifically, blokes.

'Tactile fabrics, like lace, leather or fur can stimulate the production of pleasure-giving endorphins when we touch them,' Dr Samuel Broadbent of the University of Sussex told me. It must follow, then, that if we wear fabrics which are fun to touch, the toucher is left with pleasurable associations. It's basically like a love spell! Huzzah!

A straw poll of my male friends confirmed this. 'I love it when a woman wears something fluffy,' one of them told me. 'It's like cuddling a really sexy teddy bear.' When I mentioned leather, he glazed over a bit.

Fortunately, the autumn/winter collections heavily feature these types of fabric. As well as treating myself to a limited edition LeFrequelle leather crop top (because who needs to eat or pay rent, right?), I'll be dusting off my vintage, cropped, faux-fur jacket in the hopes of attracting some loving caresses. Wish me luck!

There was a moment of silence where Wyn and I just looked at each other. I held my breath.

'That must be the single worst piece of journalism I've ever had the misfortune to encounter,' Wyn said eventually.

'I love her!' I leapt to Veronica's defence, thinking of how, when I'd imagined my London persona, she'd been quite a lot like Veronica Bailey.

'I'm sure she's got many redeeming qualities, darling, but the piece I just read was total bilge. We do not dress ourselves to attract the attention of men. Clothes should be jolly. And comfy!' She gestured at her turquoise raw-silk kaftan with a flourish.

'Fashion is supposed to be painful,' I retorted, thinking of Victoria Beckham in her six-inch heels and eye-wateringly tight jeans.

'Says who?' Wyn asked. She was less cross now. She seemed like she was genuinely intrigued. She was gazing at me intently, as though I was one of her documentaries.

'Well, no one actually says it,' I admitted. 'It's just something you . . . know.'

'I think you should look up Mary Quant,' Wyn said, lighting a cigarette and walking over to the window so she could blow the smoke outside.

'Oh yeah, who's she then?' I mumbled grumpily, frustrated that I was losing the argument.

'Fashion designer. British. Totally revolutionised women's clothes in the 1960s. She pretty much invented the miniskirt.'

'And miniskirts are comfy, are they?' I jibed.

'Well, you can run and jump and do a teddy bear roll in them. You can't say that about what women were wearing before. It was all corsets and big sticky-out dresses, darling.'

'How do you know all of this stuff?' I asked. It was so typical of Wyn to be more knowledgeable about fashion than I was, when it was supposed to be my thing.

'It's just who I am,' replied Wyn, winking at me from where she was perched on the windowsill. 'I read books, I smoke cigarettes and I know things.'

CHAPTER 7

I didn't sleep the night before my first day at college. I knew I'd set an alarm (two, in fact), but my brain kept trying to persuade me I'd somehow sleep through them both, jolting me awake any time I managed to drift off. I thought I'd feel tired by the time the alarms actually trilled, but I was buzzed as anything, leaping out of bed while trying not to knock anything over and wake Wyn.

My room was the approximate size of a cupboard. There was barely space for the single bed, chest of drawers and freestanding mirror. Several of the outfits I'd brought with me required hanging, so I had constructed a makeshift wardrobe by wedging a thick wooden stick just below the door frame. My clothes therefore formed a sort of curtain between my room and the corridor. My shoes were lined in neat rows along the skirting boards. I'd gently moved one of Wyn's paintings and used the nails in the wall to hang my necklaces.

Last night, I'd carefully ironed the 'first day at college' ensemble I'd agonised over. It was inspired by Sarah Michelle Gellar's character in *Cruel Intentions* – a tartan mini, paired with thick tights, Mary Janes, a shirt and cute little V-neck jumper. OK, so the outfit I was copying was technically a school uniform but, as SMG showed, with the right attitude and accessories you could make it look stylish.

After showering, I sat cross-legged on the tiny amount of carpet available to me and swept straighteners through my hair until it hung like a shiny sheet either side of my face. Then I applied foundation, blusher, mascara and slicked some Juicy Tubes gloss onto my lips. Perfect.

Whatever this day had in store for me, at least I looked good.

'Darling!' I heard Wyn's croaky morning voice from behind the outfit curtain. She clapped as I emerged and said, 'Look at you!' She continued, 'You simply MUST have breakfast before you go.' Then, 'I absolutely insist!' when I shook my head.

I felt sick, but forced down a few bites of toast and gulps of tea.

'Now, you know where you're going?'

'District line to Earls Court then change to a Wimbledon train for Fulham Broadway,' I parroted dutifully.

'Very good. And then it's only a few minutes' walk, as you know. Right. Now I'm satisfied that you're set for the day, I am going back to bed. See you later.' She bent to place a kiss on my forehead before floating off down the hallway.

Wyn was a freelance editor, which meant some days she had to go into an office and others she could pick her own hours, going through manuscripts in her armchair. She was a night owl, often working until well after midnight, and was notoriously grumpy before noon. I hadn't expected her to wake up early on my first day. I was touched.

I couldn't believe how busy everything was at the station. It was a battle just to get onto the platform and then, when the train arrived at Ealing Broadway, the end of the line, it seemed like hundreds more people got off it than there was room for. They just kept coming, like a tidal wave. I didn't so much walk into the carriage as I was carried by the crowd. There were people pushed right up against the doors and windows and I was crushed on every side by human bodies. All I kept thinking was, *How am I going to get off?* and, *I really hope this isn't messing up my hair and make-up.* No one else was acting like it was even slightly weird.

I put on my headphones and played my All Saints CD, skipping to their version of 'Under the Bridge'. I preferred it to the Red Hot Chilli Peppers' original. Not that I'd ever admit that publicly, of course. I focused on the melodies to try and distract from the whole giant, surreal adrenaline rush that was this journey. I couldn't believe people did this every day (and that one of those people was now me).

Fortunately, the next train, to Fulham Broadway, was quieter. I checked my reflection in the train window, stopping slightly so I could see myself. I smoothed my hair and ran my fingers under my eyes, seeing that the heat from the last train had made my mascara run slightly. I had a sense I was being watched and looked up to see a man smirking at me from further along the carriage. I felt stupid and vain, then. Embarrassed. It was a relief when I could step onto the platform, away from his judgment.

As I turned into the road where college was, I saw lots of people my age milling around on the steps outside, looking as nervous as I felt. It was obvious from their body language that they weren't quite sure what they were supposed to be doing. It was comforting, in a way. We were all in the same boat, after all.

There were tables set up in the entrance hall with smiling people behind them wearing badges reading 'Ask me anything'. I giggled to myself, as I imagined going up to them and asking what the meaning of life is.

That's when I saw him. It was only a glimpse, at first. My attention was caught by the way the overhead lights reflected off his dark, impossibly thick hair. *What I wouldn't give for hair that shiny*, I thought.

He was frowning at a piece of paper in front of him, apparently deep in concentration, so I gave myself permission to continue to stare. He had brown skin, high cheekbones and thick eyebrows. There was something kind of . . . noble about his face. That was the only way I could describe it.

He was wearing a white shirt, rolled up at the sleeves to reveal a watch with a simple leather strap. He wasn't what Rhys would call a 'chunky watch wanker', then. Rhys said you could tell a lot about a bloke from his watch . . .

Oh, god, Rhys . . .

I knew I hadn't done anything wrong, technically. I was only looking. No one had to know how my heart was thumping away in my chest, so loud I was surprised everyone around me couldn't hear it. No one had to know that my stomach was doing backflips and my throat felt like it was going to leap out of my neck. No one had to know the extent to which I physically . . . yearned to be closer to the shiny-haired fittie.

But I knew. And I also felt certain that it meant trouble.

CHAPTER 8

The first morning of college involved meeting our tutors and getting a feel for the place, which should have been easy enough. I had the additional task of trying to find someone to talk to, though. This proved more difficult than I'd expected, since quite a few of the people on my course knew each other from school. Cliques were obviously already formed. Everyone seemed to be avoiding catching my eye.

At lunchtime, I stood in the food hall trying to look out for anyone who might feel as isolated as I did. Anyone standing on the periphery nervously shifting from foot to foot, like I was.

I was dressed wrong, which was mortifying. Everyone else was in jeans and sweatshirts. They appeared casual, but I'd read enough fashion magazines to recognise the unique way designer denim is cut and the small details that mark out expensive 'lounge wear'. All the girls looked like Paris Hilton when she was getting off a plane. Informal, but still immaculate. I was tarted up to a ridiculous extent by comparison. It was strange to, on the one hand, feel as though I stuck out like a sore thumb, but on the other, to be totally ignored by everyone apart from the tutors. Conspicuous but invisible at the same time.

I was trying to orient myself as I took in the 'ra-ra yah-yah' sounds these south-west London people made as they chattered away. It's weird how differences in accent take a while to tune into. It was almost like they were speaking a different language, at first.

There was one girl who was particularly loud, with the kind of voice that cuts through the air like a drill. She was tall and slim, with tonnes of fine, almost-white-blonde hair which was obviously natural rather than dyed. She was beautiful, in a conventional sort of way – she had big blue eyes and a strong nose with freckles across the bridge. But there was something about her which signalled coldness. I couldn't explain exactly why, but she didn't look like she was thinking anything kind.

I quickly learnt her name was Sophia and watched as others flocked around her like bees around a sunflower.

'How was Saint Tropez, Soph?' asked a girl with dark hair.

'Ghastly,' she replied. 'Full of chavs, these days. Mummy says they're going to sell up and get a holiday property somewhere more exclusive, next year.'

'How dreadful for them, to have to go to all that bother,' replied the dark-haired girl, as though the 'chavs' had done it on purpose, just to inconvenience Sophia's family. There was no way I was even going to attempt a conversation with these people.

'Make way!' boomed a voice from behind them. A guy who was ninety-five per cent limbs and zero per cent coordination flopped himself down on the chair next to Sophia. He put his arm around her neck and left it there, in a possessive sort of way. Suddenly, he looked up.

'What are you staring at?' he demanded, looking directly at me. Everyone at their table also turned to gawp in my direction.

'Nothing!' I exclaimed, hating myself for how panic made my voice squeaky.

'Nuuuuuu-theeeeeeen!' the boy crowed, mimicking the way the word sounded in my South Walian accent. There was laughter from the assembled mob, who seemed to have doubled in size in the past three seconds.

Sophia looked me up and down, taking in my try-hard ensemble, a glint in her eye.

'And who might you be?' she asked, in a way that somehow managed to convey a complete lack of interest in my reply.

'My name's Cerys, nice to meet you.' I thought maybe if I pretended this was a usual sort of introduction then it would magically turn into one. 'You're Sophia, aren't you? I heard—'

'You "hewered"?' said Sophia, snorting. 'I'm sorry, are you trying to speak or dislodge some phlegm?'

I turned on my heel, not sure where I was going but certain I had to get away from them as quickly as possible. I felt something hit the back of my head as I left. There was an explosion of laughter and I caught bits of sentences they didn't even bother to whisper.

'What is she wearing?'

'Why does she talk like that?'

'What a fucking freak show.'

I walked out of the building. I felt a small jolt of excitement as I walked out of the front door. Being allowed to leave at lunchtime after so many years at school was a thrill, even under the circumstances. Eventually, I found a small patch of grass and a wooden bench at the side of the road and slumped down onto it.

I knew about bullying, obviously. I watched *Hollyoaks* just like everyone else. Yet, somehow, I'd always believed it was a thing that happened to other people. I had been pretty popular at school. Going out with a boy two years above who also happened to be captain of the rugby team helped. I was clever enough, but not so clever that I was thought of as a swot. I was also always getting detentions for customising my uniform. The sum of me had added up to cool, back in Wales.

But, as I was learning, cool isn't a universal concept. In fact, it was very much dependent on context. What made you popular in Llangunnor could make you a target in Chelsea.

I heard the distinctive trill of my Nokia 3310 – the two shrill double beeps which signalled the arrival of a text. I scrambled around in my bag and eventually found it.

Hope ur havin a brill 1st day.
Call me l8r. R xxx

I badly wanted to call Rhys in that moment. I'd tell him my London adventure wasn't going as well as I'd hoped. That I wasn't prancing along the pavement looking glamorous and stylish, off to drink a cocktail with three equally glitzy friends in tow, like Carrie Bradshaw. That the Tube was crowded and stinky and the people were rude and I didn't understand the rules of this strange new land in which I found myself. That I felt small and scared.

The thing that stopped me was knowing exactly what he'd say. He'd tell me to come back home. Not the true home I'd found at Wyn's. My actual home. And the worst thing was, the way I felt right in that second, I might have been tempted.

I flung the phone back into my bag and shook my head from side to side. I was being ridiculous. I'd only been in London for a bit more than a week, and in college for less than a day. This had been my dream for as long as I could remember. And I wasn't going to let some stuck-up cow ruin it for me.

I squared my shoulders, lifted my chin and began walking back in the direction of college. I was concentrating so hard on moving like a confident person, I didn't see the man coming out of the sandwich shop and we collided on the pavement.

'Shit!' I exclaimed, as I watched his tiny cardboard cup flip in the air and spatter his white shirt with hot brown liquid.

I was too embarrassed to look at whoever I'd just accidentally assaulted in the face, so I focused on their hands as they brushed at the stain. Wait. I'd seen that watch before. I looked up. It was him – the mysterious hottie I'd noticed at induction.

Even when wincing as the coffee soaked through the thin fabric of his shirt and (no doubt) scalded his skin, he looked completely gorgeous. Like, difficult-to-believe-he-was-real attractive.

OK, pull yourself together, Cerys, I told myself as I dared to look him in his eyes. They were deep brown and almond-shaped, with warm flecks of amber around his irises.

'I am so sorry!' I said, panting through a combination of embarrassment and, if I was honest with myself, lust.

'These things happen,' he replied, raising an eyebrow, which only made him look hotter. His voice was deep and he was well spoken, but not nasally posh in the way Sophia and her hideous friends were. There was a tinge of some kind of accent which definitely wasn't British. I couldn't have said exactly where it was from though.

'Can I . . . buy you another coffee?'

'I think another shirt would be a more appropriate offer, but in either case the answer is no. It's fine.'

'Oh. Ha ha!' I was giggling. Which was ridiculous. Especially in light of the fact that he remained stony-faced. 'Did I . . . see you at college earlier?' I asked, desperate to make some kind of connection but at the same time furious with myself for continuing to blather like an idiot.

'You attend Fulham Arts?' He batted my question back at me. He had a formal way of speaking which should have been strange, but on him was intriguingly sexy. It kind of reminded me of Mr Darcy in that TV series Mam was obsessed with a few years back.

'Yes!' My voice came out about three octaves higher than usual. 'Well. It's my first day, actually.'

I waited for him to say, 'me too!' and then to tell me what course he was studying. He looked a bit older than me, but I knew the college hosted some classes for university students and even postgrad courses. There was a moment of awkward silence. I held my breath.

'Then you should probably be getting back,' he said.

By the time I'd drawn breath to reply he was halfway down the road, striding away purposefully on his long legs in the opposite direction to the college.

CHAPTER 9

'It was fabulous! I absolutely love it here! I've made loads of friends already!' I told Rhys when he called me later that evening.

I was lying, but what else could I say? 'Actually, boyfriend who is desperate to get me back to Wales as soon as possible, I hate it here and I'm pretty sure I've crashed onto the radar of the meanest girl in the world. Which obviously means my dreams of escaping to London, which I've spent hours talking to you about, were stupid.' Not likely.

Even if he didn't beg me to get on the next train back to Llangunnor, he'd still worry about me. Better to pretend. Who knew – maybe if I pretended for long enough everything *would* eventually become fabulous?

'Aw, that's great. I'm happy for you. Tell me about your new friends.'

I knew Rhys well enough by now to know what he was really asking – 'are there any boys on your course?'

'Well, uhm. There's Sophia. She's really . . . tall. And her parents own a holiday home in Saint Tropez!' I replied.

'Ooooh, fancy!' said Rhys. 'And what about Saturday, ready for your new job?'

I'd been so wrapped up in all the college drama I'd barely thought about my new job working in a café not far from Wyn's, so his question took me by surprise.

'Well, you know. I was a waitress all summer back ho . . . back there. How different can it be?' I wondered aloud.

'Be careful, with all those London men eyeing you up.' Something about how he said it, in a sort of disjointed way which suggested he'd been waiting to get that particular sentence out since the beginning of our conversation, really irritated me.

'There's no law against looking,' I replied huffily, as much to reassure myself that my feelings towards the mysterious stranger I'd poured coffee over earlier that day were no big deal.

'I don't like the thought of it. You're a beautiful girl, Cerys. Everyone's going to want to get their hands on you and I'm not there to protect you.'

'I don't need protecting, Rhys. I'm not some precious princess with no choice in her own destiny.'

'I know! I didn't mean it like that. I just know what men are like. Speaking of which . . . Mum's out right now and I'm feeling . . . lonely. Want to tell me what you're wearing?'

'Eww. No, we are NOT doing phone sex, Rhys.'

'I should hope not!' Wyn's voice interrupted from behind the garment curtain.

'Wyn! Are you earwigging my conversation?'

'Hard not to, darling. You talk so loud on that thing I'm sure the neighbours heard it.'

I sighed. 'Got to go,' I said to Rhys, before hanging up and flinging my mobile on the bed so hard it bounced.

'Still' – Wyn's face appeared between two of my tops – 'good to hear you've had such a splendid first day at college. Well done, darling.'

The rest of the week passed in much the same way. My course was interesting enough and my tutors were friendly, but my days were overshadowed by the fear of drawing the attention of Sophia and her gang.

They were even worse than my first impressions of them could have prepared me for. They seemed to be vile to anyone who wasn't in their circle, but they made a special effort for me. It was all so immature. I'd always been under the impression that people grew out of this kind of behaviour by the time they got past GCSEs, but apparently not.

Their childishness should have made them easier to deal with, but it didn't. Maybe it was because everything and everyone was new. I probably would have been floundering a bit anyway, while I found my feet. They just made everything ten times harder than it needed to be.

I quickly learnt how to make myself quieter and smaller. I dressed in my jeans and a different baggy top each day. I left college grounds wherever possible. I kept my head down – literally – as I walked the corridors between classes. Several times, I thought about how if Rhys, or Da, or anyone from back in Wales could see me acting so apologetically, they wouldn't recognise me. I barely recognised myself.

I told myself it was just a 'holding phase'. At some point, I'd work out how to be better, how to usher in the real Cerys. I'd speak up and make friends and do all the other things I'd imagined myself doing at college. But for now, it was about survival and staying off the radar.

Each evening I'd come home and lie to Wyn about what a brilliant day I'd had. I even made up a load of bollocks about how I was 'tuning into' my most creative self, because I knew she'd love that. I wanted to make her proud and make my stay, which must have been a massive inconvenience for her (even if she never said so), worthwhile.

I was starting to feel really lonely.

Every night I lay there in my little single bed feeling like I had too many thoughts and feelings to contain them in my body. I wanted to scream, or thrash about wildly, or rip off all my clothes and run down the street naked – anything that would express my frustration. But I couldn't wake Wyn, or do anything which would alert the people around me to the fact that I might not be having the most wonderful time ever.

So, I just lay there playing the melancholy or angry songs that matched my mood on my CD Walkman, staring at the green walls or the white ceiling until I was so exhausted I passed out. I found a new appreciation for the song 'Go Let It Out' by Oasis.

If only she could, I thought miserably.

Perhaps there'd be nicer people at my Saturday job. There were bound to be, I reassured myself as I made my way to the Sunny Side Up café. Wyn had gone to put a word in for me, after seeing they were looking for temp staff. I sent them my CV and the owner phoned to say I could start as soon as I was in London. Whether that was because they weren't particularly picky or because Wyn is the most charming person on Earth, I didn't know. My wages would just about be enough to cover my expenses while I was living there.

But what if it's the same? a voice in my head interjected. *What if this is just how London people are and you'll never fit in?* I felt unmistakeable dread brewing in the pit of my stomach.

And then I saw something which pushed all other feelings out of my heart and mind immediately. I saw him.

He was sitting at one of the small, rickety metal tables outside Sunny Side Up, his face tilted towards the weak autumn sunshine. Once again, I was struck by how his face had a sort of dignity to it, with his high cheekbones and well-defined jaw. He had a tiny cup in front of him again and appeared to be deep in thought.

God knows what compelled me to do it, but I found myself stepping into his eyeline and waving.

'Hello again!' I half-shouted, in a voice that didn't sound like mine. It was as though I wasn't in control of myself, like I had puppet strings being pulled by someone much more confident. Or stupid.

He seemed to snap out of his daydream. He cleared his throat before replying.

'Hello.'

'Did you get the stain out?' I asked.

'What?'

'Of your shirt? Remember?' I mimed spilling coffee down

my own chest, cringing at my awkwardness.

'Oh, yes. I did, thank you.' He turned his head. Seemed to want the conversation to be over.

'So . . . what are you studying?' I felt determined to try and establish a connection with this strange, cold man. I would make him thaw. One day, I might even make him smile, I promised myself.

'I'm a fine artist,' he said.

I high-fived myself. He had given up some information. I was chipping away at the crust of this aloof-but-oh-so-gorgeous person.

'Really?' I lowered myself into the chair opposite his in what I hoped was an attractive fashion, making sure to cross my legs and sit at a ninety degree angle to him. According to Veronica Bailey, that was the optimal position to make your thighs look long and slim. 'I didn't even know they did that at FA.'

'They host the occasional lecture. For degree and masters students.'

'So, is that what you were doing there the other day? Attending a lecture?'

'No. I was giving a lecture.'

'Oh! But you don't look old enough!' I exclaimed, the words out of my mouth before I had time to worry whether they sounded rude.

He didn't seem to mind. In fact, for the first time since I'd known him, he smiled. It totally transformed his face. Suddenly he looked mischievous and kind of impish.

'I'm not, really. The education system is a bit different where I'm from. They asked me to present on—'

'Oi! Are you Cerys?' A woman the shape and colour of a boiled ham stepped out of the door of Sunny Side Up, wiping her hands on an apron tied around her waist. I nodded.

'Well, you're late.'

'Sorry!' I scuttled inside for my induction, waving goodbye vaguely in his direction.

'This is Alice,' the scary ham woman said, pointing to a girl standing to attention behind the rows of cakes and buns displayed on the gleaming glass counter. 'She'll show you the ropes. Any questions, I'll be in the back office doing the accounts.' Then she disappeared through a doorway hung with strings of beads.

Alice was really pretty in a kind of no-effort way. She had mid-length dark hair pulled back into a thick ponytail, pale skin, little rosebud lips and insanely long eyelashes. She reminded me a bit of Snow White.

'Hey!' She smiled as I made my way behind the counter. 'Welcome to Sunny Side Up, Ealing's answer to Central Perk! Think of me as your Gunther.' She did jazz hands as she said this and wiggled her eyebrows. I laughed, relieved she seemed so warm.

'I guess that makes me Rachel Green?' I asked, really liking the idea. Rachel was cute and funny and into fashion. Plus, everyone fancied her.

'Oooh, what a lovely accent!' Alice replied. It didn't seem like she was being sarcastic. 'Whereabouts in Wales are you from?'

I breathed out. At least she recognised my twang and didn't just think I sounded weird. 'Llangunnor. It's near Carmarthen.' I told her.

'I have some family in Swansea,' Alice said.

'Oh, right! Yeah, that's not too far!' I knew I sounded too enthusiastic, but it was just so lovely to have a conversation with someone around my age who wasn't tormenting me.

'Are you new to London?'

'Yes. I'm living with my aunt in Ealing. I've only been here a couple of weeks.'

'Let me know if you want me to show you around. I'm at uni in Central but I was born and bred in Ealing. It's my old stomping ground.'

'Thanks!'

'Have you ever waitressed before?'

'Yeah, I had a Saturday job waitressing back in Llangunnor.'

'Then this will be a total doss. Don't worry about Sally' – she indicated the beaded curtain – 'she's a bit . . . let's call her "brusque" . . . but she's actually not a bad boss. Now, let me show you how to use the till.'

Alice was right – I caught on quickly and was soon taking orders and ferrying plates of food from kitchen to customer.

By the time I went to wipe down the tables outside, he had gone.

CHAPTER 10

Alice asked me if I wanted to get something to eat after our shift.

'I know it's a weird time,' she said, 'but we work through lunch and there's ages until dinner. So I usually end up eating about four. I call it dunch. Or linner.'

'Yeah, sure,' I replied, trying to sound nonchalant. Trying not to let on how delighted I was to be invited to any kind of social occasion so I didn't come off like a sad act.

We walked to a place about five minutes away that did tacos. Alice's favourite. Of course, I had to pretend I knew what they were and that I'd had them before, bluffing my way through the process of ordering. When they arrived they were basically like a giant crisp filled with meat. They were delicious.

'What made you decide to come to London?' Alice asked.

'Lots of things. Actually, I think I first got the idea from my nain,' I told her.

'And nain means grandma, am I right?' Alice checked.

'Yeah.'

'Did she live in London, then?'

'No. She'd never even visited.' Alice looked confused and

I realised I'd have to elaborate. I didn't mind, though. It was nice to have someone show any sort of interest in me.

'She died when I was thirteen. She was living in a hospice and I went to visit her. And she said this thing I'll never forget. She said when you look back on your life, you realise there were all these decisions you spent ages agonising over and they didn't matter, not really. It's the little choices. The ones you make in a split second that make the difference.'

'Well, that's an incredibly wise thing to say,' said Alice. 'Did she give you any examples?'

'She met my taid – that means grandfather – because she randomly decided to pop into a bakery and treat herself to an iced bun. Taid was in there getting a pie for his dinner. That bakery wasn't even on her usual route through town, she said. She decided to go a different way because the sun was shining more down that side street.'

Those were the last words my nain said to me before she died. I remember her looking so tiny and frail, propped up on a mountain of pillows, drips pushed into the thick blue veins in her bony, sparrow-like hands.

I can't remember exactly what illness she had. Just that it was some sort of cancer and that it killed her quickly. Mam said we should be grateful for that, because some people live like this – the strange, painful, half-an-existence my nain was living – for years. And she wouldn't have wanted that. She was a proud woman, Mam said.

'But moving to London is a massive decision, no?' Alice's voice dragged me out of the memory. 'I mean, fair play to you.

I'm not sure I could have moved so many miles away from home at sixteen.'

'Yeah, it was.' I laughed. Not because it was funny, but because Alice couldn't possibly know how big a choice it was and how true her words were. London was everything my life had been building up to.

'What Nain said made me think . . . how can you have your fair crack at those tiny, life-changing moments when there's only about seven corners in your little village to turn? We only had one bakery you could "pop into". I felt like I would be going to same places and meeting the same people for ever until I was a wizened-up old lady like her, on my death bed.'

'I see. Yeah, I totally get that. The last person I went out with, I only met her because a mate of mine had blocked her sink in halls and I'm handy with a spanner, so I offered to go round and have a look.'

'Yeah, see? Imagine if you were less kind, you'd never have met . . . her.'

It was so strange to actually say it. I wasn't homophobic, but I also didn't know anyone who was gay. Until now. This was exactly how I thought London would be. I was out having exotic food, at a non-designated meal time, with a lesbian! Check me out!

Oh, though. What if Alice thought this was a date? I didn't want to lead her on. I also didn't want to sound up myself by assuming she fancied me. Could you even be just friends with a lesbian? *Adept* had done a feature once about whether men and women could be platonic, or whether one always secretly fancied the other. Did the same rules apply?

'I don't think this is a date,' Alice said, reading my mind. 'You don't have to worry.'

'I wasn't worried,' I lied. Then, when she raised an eyebrow at me, 'Actually, I was a bit.'

'Of course you would be. If I was a man, you'd wonder if I fancied you. If I had an ulterior motive for being your friend. And you are very beautiful.' I blushed at the compliment. 'But just so you know, you're not my type. I like women who are a bit more . . . sturdy. You have a sort of ethereal quality about you. Plus, you're obviously straight.'

'Glad we got that sorted.' I pretended to wipe my brow. 'Did you know immediately I wasn't gay? Is it true you have gaydar?'

'I mean, I can't speak on behalf of all gay people, obviously,' Alice said, 'but sometimes you do just know. And you definitely give off very heterosexual vibes. But I think the whole gaydar thing is something of an urban myth. Anyway, the point is, we're friends.'

Friends. She'd said the word. I'd done it. I'd made a friend. In that moment, I couldn't have been happier.

Meeting Alice gave me a new energy. I really and truly felt like everything was going to be OK. If Alice liked me, then that, by definition, must mean that I was likeable. For the first time in ages, I felt optimistic.

I tried to hold onto that confidence in the weeks that followed. I caught the occasional glimpse of Hot Lecturer and his shiny hair at college, but he never came to the café on Saturday again. I couldn't speak to him if there was a chance one of my bullies would show up and embarrass me, so I just watched him from afar. Whenever there was a dull bit in one of my classes, I'd have daydreams about what I'd say to him once Sophia and her mates got bored of tormenting me and I was finally free. It would have to be something devastatingly clever and funny. I wanted him to fancy me, even if I did have a boyfriend.

I held onto my belief that if I didn't react Sophia would get bored and the bullying would stop. I tried not to flinch when things were thrown at me from behind, or I heard whispers and laughter following me as I walked between classes.

I started thinking of week days as just time between Saturdays. Shifts at Sunny Side and dunch with Alice afterwards were the memories I clung onto and the thing I looked forward to. They were the only times when I felt like myself, when I wasn't lying to Wyn and Rhys about how wonderful college was, or trying to think of new ways to become invisible.

Most of all, I tried not to show how scared and on edge I felt whenever Sophia and her mates were nearby. If I just kept pretending nothing was wrong, they would stop. I had to believe that, because there were no other options.

One Monday morning in October, I saw Sophia striding down the corridor straight towards me, flanked on either side by her mean-girl sidekicks Tara and Jasmine.

I expected a bitchy remark or another attempt to humiliate me. Perhaps she'd talk in my earshot again about my clothes being 'gyppo' and how it was ridiculous for me to think I had a future in fashion. Or maybe she'd do her 'hilarious' impression of my accent, which was actually just a series of gormless-sounding grunts.

I was determined not to let her know how much she'd got to me, so I stood with my chin jutting out, hoping she couldn't see the slight tremble I could feel vibrating through my hands.

'We've been talking,' Sophia said in her nasal tone as she reached me, 'and we've decided we haven't been fair to you.'

This knocked me off kilter, totally. I glanced around, expecting Spencer to be creeping up behind me with a tin of dog food, ready to pour it down my top like in that film *Never Been Kissed*. But everyone was just walking around as usual, ignoring us. No one seemed to be preparing themselves for a theatre show.

'OK . . .' I replied warily.

'Can we start again?' Sophia said, blinking the long lashes that framed her large round blue eyes and smiling.

I wanted to scream at her, to say, 'No we CAN'T fucking "start again"! Not after you ruined one of my favourite jumpers by "accidentally" spilling glue on it and spread horrible rumours about me and basically made my life a living hell. Who do you think you are, to even ask me that?' But I wasn't brave enough, so I said, 'Uhm . . . sure.'

'Great!' All three of them were smiling at me now, looking at me adoringly like I was a kitten or something. 'So you'll come to Spencer's house party on Friday, yah?'

I'd heard them talking about Spencer's parties before, during the snatches of conversations I had caught as I tried to scuttle past them unnoticed between classes. The parties were apparently epic.

I felt a bit uneasy – of course I did – but wasn't this what I'd come to London for? To experience something new and exciting? Maybe my new friendship with Alice meant I was on a winning streak. Maybe I could make Sophia like me and then I wouldn't have to spend my whole time at college trying to disappear. Maybe, next time Wyn asked me how my day was, I wouldn't have to lie.

So, despite the twisting in my guts, I said yes.

CHAPTER 11

I tried on every item of clothing I owned, attempting to strike the right balance between 'refined enough to compete with super-rich Chelsea people' and 'not trying too hard'. I'd crashed and burned with my outfit choice for the first day of college, so I didn't quite trust my own judgment.

I had a sparkly silver mini-dress with fringing at the bottom that could work if it was super glam, but I wasn't sure if people here got dressed up for house parties here. I could play it safe with black trousers and a halter top, but that's the kind of thing Mam would probably wear if she ever went to a party. Which she didn't. Obviously.

I sighed, frustrated. It was so important I got this right.

I resented Sophia for putting me in a position where I had to suck up to her, but it was one of those things. And anyway, I was desperate for any kind of party, at this point. Back in Wales, I went out every Saturday night, without fail. It was always Rhys, me and a few others. Rhys had said to me once that we were the LPC – Llangunnor's Premier Couple. We were certainly the glue that held our little social group together.

Rhys always made me drink pints of cider. I hated the taste

of it, but he said it would help us get a buzz on. Then we'd get a cab to a club in Carmarthen to dance. That, for me, was the real buzz. It was the one time during the week when I could forget everything else – that Mam was doing my head in, that Rhys was pressuring me to 'settle down', that I felt like I'd been born in the wrong place and was so desperate to escape I could scream – and just have fun. Rhys would keep trying to drag me to the bar to do shots, but I'd stay on the dance floor all night, right under the disco ball. Nothing mattered in those few hours but the beat of the music.

I missed dancing so much. I hoped people would dance tonight. Even more, I hoped the music would be decent.

I sat cross-legged on my bed, put in my earphones and played 'Sun is Shining' by Bob Marley vs Funkstar De Luxe. That track never failed to relax me.

Forcing myself not to think too much, I pulled out a denim bandeau top I'd made out of one leg of an old pair of jeans. Maybe that with a miniskirt and boots? Yes, that was it. Thank you, Bob and Funkstar. Even if it was totally wrong, the outfit would show off my toned stomach and my long legs. Three reasons to be confident.

It was already dark when I left Wyn's. On the Tube, I stood in the space between the seats, holding on to the handrail. I caught sight of my reflection in the window of the train. I looked how I always imagined I would when I was dreaming of coming here. Adult. Sexy. Kind of like Christina Aguilera (if you squinted). I felt a little excited shiver travel up my spine.

Spencer lived on the Fulham Road, not far from college.

Sophia had pointed out the way as we left college and texted me the address. It was a tall white building with steps leading up to a glossy black front door (which was TOTALLY Carrie Bradshaw). I squared my shoulders and rang the bell.

Sophia answered. She was wearing low-slung jeans, a silky top with thin straps and platform sandals. If I didn't know, I would have guessed her age at about twenty-five. I instantly felt childish and clueless by comparison. I thought about making a dash for it. Telling her I'd forgotten something and would be back later. Going home to change. But instead I forced myself to smile and put my shoulders back like I thought a self-assured person might.

'Hi, doll!' she screeched, wrapping her slender arms around me. I had to stop myself flinching. 'We're in the basement, follow me.'

The hallway was vast, with black and white tiles on the floor that reminded me of a chessboard. There was a spiral staircase leading upwards and then another, set further back, twisting downwards.

The basement was the size of Wyn's entire flat. There was a huge fridge in one corner, open to reveal rows of champagne like something out of *Absolutely Fabulous*. There was also a massive barrel filled with ice and bottles of beer. The lights were dim and someone was standing at a turntable, playing house music I didn't recognise. The space in front of him was empty, but I hoped it might become a dance floor later. At the other end of the room was a long couch, on which a group of girls were huddled. They were all dressed identically to Sophia.

All six of them seemed to spin round then face me, look me up and down with matching disapproving frowns and then plaster on smiles in one synchronised movement.

'Make room for Cerys!' said Sophia. 'Tara, get her a champers, will you?' A flute appeared in my hand seconds later, as I lowered myself nervously into the space they'd made for me on the sofa, right in the middle.

'Now, introductions! Tara and Jasmine you know, of course. This is Arabella, Tilly, Verity and Frances, but everyone calls her Binky.'

I turned to each side to wave. It felt stupid. 'Nice to meet you,' I said.

'Oh!' either Tilly or Binky (it was already difficult to tell them apart) exclaimed. 'What a delightfully . . . odd way of speaking you have!'

I blinked, unsure whether I'd just been insulted or not. The others just stared at me with curiosity, but also somehow lazily, as though I was a mildly interesting artefact in a museum.

It was so awkward, I knocked back my champagne in one, just for something to do. It tasted sour, like bad breath.

'Oooh! Someone's on a mission!' Sophia observed.

Just then, there was an explosion of noise and movement at the bottom of the stairs. Spencer had appeared with a gang of lads, all as floppy-haired and lanky as he was.

'STEWFACE, YOU RUDDY OLD TWAT!' Spencer was shouting to one of them, who smiled and rolled his eyes simultaneously. They all made their way over to the barrel, grabbing beers, before sauntering across to us.

'How's my gorgeous girl?' Spencer sat on the end of the couch and draped his arm around Sophia, so her neck was squeezed into the crook of his elbow. She didn't look comfortable but she seemed delighted by his attention, nonetheless.

'Just getting lubricated,' Sophia replied, holding up her flute of champagne and taking a delicate sip.

'I bet you are, you horny tart,' Spencer replied, and got a playful slap in return.

Everyone else seemed to be watching Sophia and Spencer, waiting for permission to speak. There were about twelve of us by this stage, all huddled around the couple, watching them as though they were on TV. It was really weird, but it occurred to me that I was used to being one half of the couple everyone congregated around. I felt like a tourist, seeing what it was like on the other side of the fence.

'Taffy No-Tits!' Spencer foghorned in my direction as he suddenly noticed me. 'So glad you could join us!'

I folded my arms over my chest self-consciously.

Spencer leant forward and slapped my hand away. 'Nothing to be ashamed of there! You know they say more than a handful's a waste? Well, I say more than a MOUTHFUL's a waste! HAR HAR HAR,' he boomed. Everyone joined in, creating a hideous cacophony of fake laughter.

I felt like I might cry, but also knew I'd have to die of humiliation if I did. So, to show him I could take a joke I said, 'Luckily for you, Sophia feels the same way about cocks.'

For a split second, Spencer looked furious. The group held its collective breath. Then he laughed again, a little less loudly.

He leant in again towards me. 'Feisty. I like that,' he whispered and winked.

To my relief, the bubble of tension had burst and the chat turned to other things. Over time, the group got separated by gender. Girls on the sofa, boys standing by the fridge. I was stuck discussing Binky's new car (a gift for her seventeenth birthday from her parents, which had a personalised number plate), Tilly's 'nightmare' trying to find a certain Prada knapsack and details of Jasmine's long-distance romance with a man she had met in Provence.

Part of me was uncomfortable, knowing how little I had to add to these conversations. Yet in another way, it was just nice to be out. The general hubbub of the party – the clinking of glasses and the laughter set against the backdrop of some anonymous dance track was soothing. I just let myself sort of melt into it, sinking back into the cushions as I did so.

I became aware of sudden movement as Sophia and Tilly leapt up from the sofa and, linking arms, made their way to the staircase. 'Just popping to powder our noses!' Sophia shouted over her shoulder.

Those of us who were left sat in silence for a few excruciating beats. I didn't feel comfortable any more.

'Actually,' I said, 'I need a wee too. Back in a sec.'

I crept around the hallway, opening doors and hoping to find a bathroom behind one of them. They all led to huge rooms with high ceilings. They were all empty, with no signs that people lived in them. There were no half-read books on the coffee table. No slippers by the side of the sofa. No cat hair on anything. It was so different to Wyn's, which was cosy and inviting.

I wondered where Spencer's parents were. Then I realised that I hadn't seen a kitchen yet and that it must be on one of the higher floors. I'd thought they must be for bedrooms because . . . well . . . bedrooms were upstairs, weren't they? But everything in this place was topsy turvy. It was like I was Alice in Wonderland.

After failing to find a toilet, I tiptoed up the spiral staircase to the next floor. I tried the handle of the first door I came to, but it was locked. Sophia's voice floated out.

'Occupied! Out in a minute!'

I heard giggles. She and Tilly must be weeing together. I felt a twinge of sadness as I wished I had a best friend to wee with.

There was a small table next to the door with a mirror above it, so I wandered over to check my make-up while I waited. I stared at my reflection, framed by all this unfamiliar poshness.

Many people had told me I was beautiful, in my life. Even Mam had, on occasion. (Although in a begrudging way, like the fact I was pretty annoyed her. Along with everything else about me.) Yet, compared with the girls I was out with tonight, I felt like the equivalent of a hand-knitted jumper with a bit of egg on the front when they were all designer blazers.

I had at least two centimetres of roots visible where I'd last had my highlights done a few months ago and split ends where I straightened so zealously. My tan looked obviously fake compared with the real versions Chelsea people picked up on their summer holidays. As much as I tried to customise my clothes so they weren't identical to the ones you saw in the windows of New Look and Dorothy Perkins, they obviously weren't designer either. How was I ever going to blend into this world?

'Thank you, sweets.' I heard Tilly's voice from behind the door. 'I mean, what is she even doing here?'

Sophia's voice replied, 'Oh god, I don't know. Spencer wanted her here tonight for some reason. Gave me a big lecture about being nicer to her. Said I should invite her.'

'Weird,' Tilly replied, with a sniff. 'I mean, she's hardly a valuable addition to the group. She's dressed like a twelve-year-old at their first disco.'

I heard movement behind the door. I didn't want to be standing there when they emerged, so I quickly ran down the staircase and across the hall. Spencer was standing at the top of the stairs leading to the basement holding two flutes of champagne, like he'd been expecting me.

'Is it true you told Sophia to invite me tonight?' I blurted, before I could stop myself.

He pretended to think about it. 'Why, yes. Now you mention it.'

'Why?' I fired back, trying to will the blood flow away from my cheeks where I could feel a humiliated blush rising.

'Isn't it obvious?' He looked me up and down leerily.

'But you're with Sophia!'

'Oh, we have a bit of fun. But she isn't my girlfriend or anything.'

'Well, I have a boyfriend,' I retorted.

'And what he doesn't know can't hurt him,' Spencer chortled.

We heard Sophia and Tilly's heels clomping down the staircase. Spencer put his arm around me and led me down the basement stairs.

'Now, there's no need for anyone to get upset,' he instructed. 'We're meant to be having fun! Here.' He held one of the glasses of champagne towards me. 'Cheers.' He touched his glass to mine before gulping some of the pale amber liquid. 'Look, Taff. Don't bring down the mood. You have to learn to laugh at yourself if you want people to like you. We can have a bit of a drink and a dance together as friends, right? There's no law against that?'

I gulped down some of my drink angrily while I tried to think of a reply. Something that would knock him off balance and wipe that stupid smirk off his face.

'There you go.' He nodded approvingly. 'Knew you were all right really. Let's dance!' he ordered, beckoning a couple of his mates to the turntable. The music seemed to have got louder. Most of the boys and a few of the girls were dancing. Spencer grabbed my hands and started spinning me in circles. Sophia and Tilly watched us from the bottom of the stairs, looking at me like they wished I would die.

Suddenly, I felt really sick.

'Spencer!' I yelled. 'Let go of me!' I needed to get out of there.

'Come on, Taff,' Spencer shouted into my ear. 'We're having fun, aren't we?' Then he pinched my bum, hard. The room started to spin. I didn't understand – I hadn't drunk that much.

I pushed him away, barged past the dancing bodies, past Sophia and up the stairs. I was desperate for fresh air. The chessboard floor rocked from side to side as I lurched across the hall. I opened the front door. I had completely forgotten there were steps there.

I felt my heel catch something and I tumbled down, desperately trying to grab the railings either side of the steps to steady myself. I only partly succeeded. I landed on the pavement on my knees and my handbag spilt open. I couldn't seem to get myself upright. I was scrabbling around on the floor, trying to gather up the lip gloss and keys scattered around me.

I heard laughter coming from above. Blearily, I looked up. All of them were standing in the doorway, watching me, in hysterics. Their faces looked distorted and grotesque as they cackled. Not one of them came down the stairs to help me as I flailed about on the pavement. It was like being trapped in a nightmare. I wished it was a dream. I pinched the skin on my arm, in case it would make me wake up. It didn't.

'Say cheese, Taff!' I heard Spencer taunting. I looked up, saw he was pointing a camera at me. I raised my hand, tried to cover my face, but it was too late. The flash hurt my eyes.

Somehow, I summoned the strength to stand. Then I stumbled along the pavement as fast as I could on my shaking legs. I had no idea where I was going. I just needed to get away. I could hear myself breathing heavily as I put one foot in front of the other. It took all my concentration not to veer into the road, or a hedge.

Then, darkness seemed to whoosh in from either side of my head, obscuring my vision.

Everything faded to black.

CHAPTER 12

I was startled awake by a shaft of light hitting my face as it shone through a gap in some blinds. I was lying in a bed with a hard mattress and white sheets. I knew immediately that it wasn't my own. I had absolutely no memory of how I had got there.

I tried to sit up, but my head throbbed painfully, forcing me back down onto the pillows. Tentatively, I stretched one arm out, then one leg. The other side of the vast double bed was empty and cold. I racked my brain, trying to remember anything that happened after I'd run away from Spencer's, but my mind was totally blank.

I turned my head slowly. On the bedside table was a glass of water, alongside my phone. Struggling into a sitting position, I grabbed the water and gulped it down, gratefully. Then I peered at my phone screen with one eye closed. Fourteen missed calls from Wyn. I went to dial her number, then realised that telling her I was alive but had no idea where I was might not be the best idea. I had to establish some facts before we had a conversation, but I sent her a quick text saying:

SORRY. Am fine. Call you later.

That would hopefully stop her worrying.

I looked around the room. It was large, but sparse, with slatted pine blinds and a matching chest of drawers. There was nothing at all to indicate who the room belonged to. Perhaps I was in a hotel. To my left was an open door revealing a sparkling white ensuite bathroom.

Wincing, I heaved myself out of bed and tiptoed over to the sink, daring myself to look into the mirrored cabinet above it. I looked hideous. My eyes were red and puffy and my make-up was all over my face. My hair looked like birds had been nesting in it for the past six months. I opened the cabinet. It contained some shaving foam and a razor, mouthwash, toothpaste and an electric toothbrush.

I turned towards the shower and saw just two bottles in a wire rack on the wall – a shower gel with an expensive-looking label reading 'sandalwood' in an old-fashioned script and a two-in-one shampoo and conditioner.

Reading the labels made me feel violently sick, for some reason. Like I used to feel on car journeys when I was little. I dropped to my knees, grateful that the toilet was in such close proximity as I felt vomit rising in my throat. I chundered violently and then collapsed back onto the floor, trying to get my breathing back to normal.

What the hell did I do last night?

I stayed there on the bathroom floor for what could have been anything from two minutes to two hours. Time had lost all meaning. I knew I needed to get up, but I didn't seem to be able to command my body to do anything. I felt totally numb, like when you sleep on your arm and you can't move it, but in my entire body.

Eventually, I somehow mustered the strength to stand again. I splashed my face with water, ran wet fingers through my hair and swilled out my mouth with the mouthwash. I had to make myself look as presentable as possible so Wyn wouldn't have a complete fit when I got back home. I straightened my clothes, grabbed my phone and tiptoed out of the room.

It took a while for my eyes to adjust to the darkness of the hallway. I could see what looked like the front door of a flat – it had a peephole and chain at the top but was otherwise completely featureless – to my right. Straight ahead was another door like the one I'd just stepped though, slightly ajar.

I had a choice. I could either run to the front door, escape, and spend the rest of my life wondering whose flat I'd woken up in, or I could open the other door and find out. Option one was probably safer. I knew that, logically. Yet, another more persuasive part of me just had to know.

Careful not to make a sound, I pushed the door in front of me gently with one finger. It was a combined kitchen and living space with shiny wooden floors, a large window at one end and a balcony beyond. It looked as though it was early morning, but the sun hadn't yet come round to this part of the building, meaning it hadn't disturbed the person sleeping under a blanket on the sofa. Poking out one end I could see large, slender brown feet. At the other was a familiar mass of shiny dark hair.

It's weird what your brain does in moments of shock.

The first thing I thought was, *how does he keep his hair that shiny when he uses a two-in-one shampoo and conditioner?* That was before my mind became occupied with the more obvious questions of how and why I'd made it into Hot Lecturer's flat.

I felt like I was going to collapse again and stumbled slightly, grabbing the doorframe to steady myself. The noise woke him. He turned his head, saw me, then sat up very slowly. He was wearing a pair of grey jogging bottoms and a T-shirt, which he yanked down self-consciously. He didn't break eye contact with me the whole time, as though I was a dangerous snake who could strike at any moment.

He held both his hands up, palms facing forwards. 'It's OK,' he said, 'you're safe. Please come and sit down.' He gestured at an armchair opposite the sofa. I remained totally still, staring, wanting to blink my sore eyes but scared of what would happen if I did.

He spoke again, softly. 'I know you must have lots of questions, Cerys. I will answer them as best I can. I promise you are safe. Please, sit.'

I started to walk towards the chair, still unable to take my eyes off him – and him still holding my gaze.

'Do you want a cup of tea?' he asked. I nodded. 'OK. Stay there. Try to relax.'

I felt completely disconnected from what was happening, like I was watching him on TV. I lowered myself slowly into the armchair, suddenly aware of how tiny my top and skirt were, that my belly was still on show. I picked up a cushion and hugged it against myself as I watched him put teabags and boiling water into two generic white mugs.

'I don't have milk. Sorry,' he said, as he brought them over and handed me one.

'That's OK.' The tea was more for something to do with my hands than to actually drink.

We sat in silence for a moment.

'How much do you remember?' he eventually asked.

'I . . . I remember going to Spencer's house for a party. I felt really ill all of a sudden and so I left . . . but I fell down the steps outside his house and landed on the pavement.' I glanced down at my knees; their vivid red grazes backed up my memory. 'They were . . . laughing at me. Someone took a photo. I ran away . . . Then everything went blank. The next thing I knew, I woke up here.'

'OK.' He lowered his head, staring into his mug of tea. 'I can tell you what I know and we can try and work out what happened in the intervening period.'

I dimly registered once again what a strangely formal way of talking he had. I liked it, though. Along with his accent, I'd never met anyone who spoke quite like him before.

'I went out last night at around nine o'clock to pick up some dinner. I saw you on the pavement, stumbling, looking distressed. I realised I recognised you and thought perhaps I could help. I tried to ask you what was wrong, but your speech was slurred and you were very confused. I only caught a few coherent words. You definitely said the name Spencer. Multiple times, in fact.'

I tried to remember this happening but I couldn't. It was like a whole chunk of my memory had been removed.

He went on. 'I asked you where you live. I thought I could see you back to your door. But you couldn't tell me your address and you also seemed very concerned someone you were calling "win" would be angry with you. In the end I felt I had no other choice than to bring you back here. You weren't safe out there on your own.'

'There wasn't anyone with me?'

'No.'

'I did have a couple of drinks . . . maybe three. But I have never been that drunk before. How embarrassing.'

He cleared his throat. 'Have you considered, Cerys, that it might not have been the effect of alcohol that led to your state last night?'

'What do you mean? I don't take drugs. I never have. Well, apart from the odd joint with my . . . a friend. But if anyone had offered me pills, I'd have said no. I'm sure of it.'

'Have you thought about the possibility that maybe they weren't offered to you?'

I instinctually went to deny it. Then I stopped. I made a 'wwwh' sound and then, from nowhere, I just started crying. I sobbed with great heaving gasps, like you do when you're a toddler and the sorrow feels like it's too much for your tiny body to contain.

He gently put his cup onto the coffee table between us and moved so he was standing to the side of me. He patted me awkwardly on the shoulder for a few moments and, when that failed to stop my tears, he squatted down beside me and put an arm around my shoulder. I turned and buried my face into his T-shirt.

And even though I was clearly in the middle of some kind of nervous breakdown, it didn't stop me from noticing how good he smelt or how wonderful it felt to be touching him. For the first time in a long time, I felt safe.

I wept until my whole body felt wizened, as though I'd squeezed out every drop of moisture within me and there was no more left. The whole time, he just stayed next to me with his arm around my shoulder, not speaking, letting me use his T-shirt as a giant hanky. Somehow, he seemed to know exactly what I needed – to cry it out.

Finally, when my breathing had slowed down a bit, I said, 'I need to call my Auntie Wyn.'

'Of course. You may use my phone, if you like.' He indicated a landline perched on a small glass side table next to the sofa.

It felt awkward to have the conversation with him in the room, but I also didn't want to use up the precious credit on my mobile. I also wanted to seem grown-up and sophisticated to him, which was difficult considering the fact that I was covered in snot, had grazed knees and generally looked (and felt) as though I'd just crawled out of a bin. Doing a sheepish apology to my auntie for not informing her of my whereabouts wasn't exactly going to make me seem sexier.

As though he could sense my thoughts, he ambled over to the kitchen area and started pottering. It was such an obvious

'I am not eavesdropping, honest' gesture, but I appreciated it. I took a deep breath and dialled.

'You can stay out as long as you like. You know that, darling. I'm not running some draconian convent! Just tell me where you are and when to expect you home. It's not much to ask. You have a mobile. A text is all I'm asking for,' said Wyn.

'I know, I'm sorry. Again,' I replied. Then, dropping my voice in the vain hope he wouldn't hear, I asked the question that had been playing on my mind. 'You didn't tell Mam, did you?'

There was a pause, which couldn't have lasted more than a few seconds but felt as though it stretched out for an eternity. 'I thought it better not to, on this occasion,' Wyn said eventually. 'But don't imagine I will hesitate to call her if this happens again. Am I making myself clear, darling?'

'Yes.' I exhaled the word in a sigh of relief.

'I'll be home . . . soon,' I promised, before hanging up.

By the time I'd replaced the receiver, he'd washed the mugs we'd been drinking out of and was drying them with a tea towel. I could see the muscles in his arms moving as he did it. God, he was so hot. And this was so not the ideal state for me to be in while in his presence.

'I should go,' I said. 'Thank you so much. For having me.' I suddenly became all awkward and formal, like he'd invited me over for a tea party.

'It was . . . Well, not my pleasure. That is the wrong way to say it. My honour, perhaps.' He smiled. 'Do you need me to come with you to the station?'

I laughed. 'I can see it from here!' I gestured out of the French windows, where the Tube sign was gleaming in the mid-morning sunshine.

'Oh. No, I meant . . . the police station.'

'What?'

'Cerys.' He abandoned the mug and tea towel and came over to me, perching himself on the opposite side of the couch. 'I suspect you had your drink spiked last night. There is a time period neither of us can account for where anything could have happened to you. You might need to be . . . checked out.'

I clocked his meaning and cringed. 'No! I feel . . . fine. I mean, OK, not fine. But . . . I'd know if anything . . . like *that* had happened . . .'

'I'm not going to tell you how you feel. But I do know a little bit about the law around this kind of thing. And if you don't make a report today it will be much harder later. If your memory did come back, and you remembered something had happened to you. Look . . .' He shifted a little further in my direction and took my hand gently, like it was a bar of soap that would slip away if he squeezed it too hard. 'I can't imagine how difficult this is for you. But I need to strongly urge you to do what's in your best interests.'

I knew he was probably right, but I also didn't feel like I could properly process anything, like I was being swept along by a wave and everything was happening too fast.

I looked down at our hands, still intertwined. His were large, with prominent knuckles and long fingers so they somehow looked both elegant and strong. Mine looked dainty by comparison.

I fought back more tears. 'OK,' I squeaked. 'But I will have to go later. I have a shift at the café and if I don't leave now I'll be late.'

'Of course.'

Something about the way he said it, his voice calm and low, his hands warm and solid around mine, made me believe it was all going to be all right.

He walked me out of his flat and into the lift. He was on the sixth floor, I noticed. Flat number 604. Once we were outside, there was a short stretch of car park which we walked across in silence. It wasn't awkward, though. I liked having him nearby.

It was only when we got to the big iron gates which made a barrier between his block of flats and the pavement that he spoke.

'Will you be OK to get home?' he asked. He'd been so kind to me today. Nothing like the frosty person I'd first met.

'Yes, I'll be fine. Thank you, errrr . . .' I touched his sleeve. He looked at me with his eyebrows raised. 'This is really embarrassing,' I continued, 'but I just realised I don't know your name.'

He looked at me for a long moment. He had a conflicted look on his face, almost as though he was considering not telling me. Finally, he said softly, 'It's Darsh.'

'Darsh.' I repeated, rolling the name around on my tongue. I'd never heard it before. 'I don't know how I'm ever going to thank you enough for what you've done for me.'

'Please,' he said. 'You don't have to thank me.' I heard a shout from further down the street, which made Darsh look up. He suddenly seemed less relaxed, pushing a button hidden in the bushes. The gates opened and he pushed me gently through.

'Take care of yourself, Cerys.' And then he turned and jogged back into the building.

CHAPTER 13

By the time I got back to Wyn's, I felt weary like I never had before. All I wanted to do was have a shower, climb into bed and sleep for a week. Unfortunately, life had other ideas.

I had half an hour until my shift at Sunny Side, so I rushed about trying to make myself vaguely presentable. Meanwhile, Wyn was following me from room to room, asking me questions I either couldn't or didn't want to answer about the night before. Did I have a good time? Where did I stay? Was I all right? Did I want some breakfast?

It's like being with Mam, I thought irritably. I came to London to escape the fussing.

I could see a series of texts had arrived from Rhys, but I didn't have the time or the energy to deal with them. I'd get through my shift and then I could think.

At Sunny Side, I plastered on a smile. I took orders, collected plates and rang cash through the till. Alice taught me how to froth milk to make a cappuccino. Everyone in London seemed to want cappuccinos constantly.

It was nice, in a way, to have these simple tasks to distract me from everything else.

During my twenty-minute break I sat at the top of the iron stairwell round the back of the café and checked my phone. There was a message on the screen telling me I'd run out of storage space and to delete some of my texts. Usually, I'd agonise over which of my ten allotted saved texts to delete for ever, but today I just erased them all. I felt too detached; too overwhelmed to care. It prompted a stream of beeping, as message after message from Rhys arrived.

At first, they were the normal sort of texts Rhys sent, asking how I was, reminding me that he loved me, to be careful and not to let any London boys look at or touch me. I hadn't been planning to, but these messages confirmed I couldn't even contemplate telling him about last night.

Then, when I hadn't replied, the tone of the texts had changed.

Why are you ignoring me?

What the fuck???

Then, something longer. An unfiltered stream which went over the 167 characters allowed for each text and arrived in chunks:

The first:

Cerys I knew this wud happen. I let u go to Ldn cos u kept on about it but I knew u wud forget about me. I know I luv u more than u ever luved me. Ur prob with sum sleazy Ldn bloke laughing about me . . .

Then:

. . . well fuck you. All I ever dun is be supportive of u. All my m8s said u wud betray me n I defended u but they wre right. U think ur so much better than me. U think ur better than us n wales . . .

Then:

. . . u think ur going to get discovered as a model or be famous. Never going to happen. Ur pathetic. I gave you everything n ur just a SLAG. I deserve better. Goodbye. Don't contact me again

I put my face in my hands, breathing heavily. I could tell he was drunk when he wrote it, but it didn't matter. The mask had slipped. He'd never called me names before. He'd never hinted that he believed he was 'letting' me go to London. I knew he was jealous, but I didn't think he'd been talking to his mates about me, accusing me of being unfaithful. There were some things you just couldn't recover from and I knew, right smack in my guts, that this was one of them.

But the worst thing was, Rhys was right, in a way. He was always more serious about our relationship than I was. I went along with it because he was exactly the sort of boy I believed I should fall in love with – he was good-looking and popular and made me laugh. Yet there was always something missing. We both knew it, I think, but we pretended like it wasn't there, hoping maybe it might go away, one day.

I hadn't cheated on Rhys, but I also hadn't thought about him – not even for a fleeting second – during the past twenty-four hours. Wasn't that kind of the same? Or at the very least a sign that things weren't OK?

And that's when it hit me. Among the mish-mash of emotions I was feeling – anger, betrayal, shock – there was one bigger than the rest, like a huge wave crashing into a shore and wiping away the marks in the sand. Relief.

I felt a touch on my shoulder which, even though it was feather-light, scared the absolute crap out of me. I jumped.

'Sorry! Didn't mean to frighten you! You looked like you were miles away.' It was Alice. I exhaled, trying to slow down my heartbeat.

'I was. What time is it?' I asked, looking at my phone and realising I'd gone five minutes over my break time. 'Shit. Shit shit shit. Sorry, Alice. I'm coming back in now.'

'Hey, it's OK. I was just coming to check if you were all right. Are you? You look a bit freaked out.' She put both her hands on my shoulders. They were comfortingly heavy and warm.

I was about to tell her everything, when Sally came crashing into view, startling us both.

'Ladies, when you've finished gossiping or snogging or whatever the hell it is I'm paying you to do back here, there are customers waiting.'

'Sorry!' we yelled in unison and hurried back to the counter.

'Tell me later,' Alice whispered.

***

At the end of our shift, we filled takeaway cups with hot chocolate and walked to a little park set back from the road. It was cold and there was a fine drizzle in the air, so it was empty apart from a woman in a bright orange bobble hat walking her tiny dog. We sat on a bench and watched the tiny dog for a bit. It was lovely, just sitting. Not talking, but not alone.

Then, after a while, I told Alice about everything I could remember from the night before.

'Fuck!' she exclaimed, when I was finished. 'Bastards.'

'Well, yeah. But I don't know why I expected anything different really. They've always been vile to me at college. Then all of a sudden it was like Sophia had a personality transplant and she's inviting me to a party. I should have seen it coming. I was an idiot, I—'

'You're being unfair on yourself,' Alice interjected. 'You're just a good person who takes others at face value. That's nothing to be ashamed of.'

'You know what they say though – fool me once, shame on you. Fool me twice . . .'

'Yeah, I know. And this Darsh guy – you know him from college too?'

'Mmm-hmm.'

Something had stopped me telling Alice too much about Darsh, aside from very brief details of how he'd rescued me the night before. I liked him being my thing. Like a safe haven away from the rest of reality.

'Oh my god, you LIKE him.' Alice had turned to face me now and was staring at the side of my head intently.

'Look, that is beside the point of this story,' I replied, sucking in my cheeks so I wouldn't smile and give myself away.

'Quite right, actually. Sorry. The point is, what are you going to do now? Doesn't seem like they should get away with it, what they've done to you. Are you going to tell the college?'

'Well, Darsh said I should go to the police. In case my drink was spiked. Plus, there's a time period I can't really remember . . .' I trailed off.

'Do you think something really bad happened?' Alice asked gently.

'Honestly? No. I totally blanked out but I also feel like I'd know. Or my body would know. And the only pain I feel is my knees and my palms, where I fell down the stairs.'

'Still, spiking someone's drink is illegal.'

'I should report it.'

'You should.'

'But maybe I'm being silly?' I argued. 'Could have been a bad reaction to the champagne. I hadn't eaten much that day. I don't want to get anyone in trouble . . .'

'What if you'd be saving someone else?' Alice asked.

'How do you mean?'

'Let's say you were spiked and it was Spencer who did it. Reporting it could stop him doing it to another girl. And who knows whether something even worse might happen to her?'

'Yeah. I know you're right. I'm a bit nervous, though. About actually going to the police station. That feels like a very serious thing to do,' I admitted.

'Cerys?'

'Yes?'

'Shall I come with you?'

'Please.'

CHAPTER 14

The wait at the police station seemed to last for an eternity. Several times on the walk there I'd wanted to turn back, convinced I was being silly.

'You can do this, Cerys,' Alice said. Then she gave me a hug. It felt lovely.

'Why are you being so nice to me?' I asked. 'You hardly know me.'

'Maybe I'm your guardian angel.'

We walked in silence for a bit. Alice seemed like she was deep in thought.

'Cerys, can I tell you something?'

'Sure.'

'I know you're freaking out, and this is not about me, but . . . OK, I have a sister . . . well, *had*, I guess. She was called Aimee. She died when she was twelve. She would have been your age, now.'

'Oh my god. I'm so sorry. That's awful,' I replied. I wasn't sure if that was the right thing to say. I'd never had anyone tell me something so terrible before.

'Thank you. I miss her every day. And I know this is a bit

weird, but something about you reminds me of her. I'm not sure what it is exactly. Same vibe. Anyway, the point is, if something like this had happened to her, I'd really want her to report it. Can you accept the advice from a . . . kind of . . . proxy big sister?'

I nodded and we walked on, me wondering how Aimee died but feeling like it wouldn't be appropriate to ask.

When we arrived, we told a bored-looking officer behind glass in reception we were there to report a possible crime. We were told to wait in a little area with hard grey plastic chairs. They were the most uncomfortable seats in the world. The station was quiet and even if I could have thought of something to say, it felt wrong to speak. Still, I was glad Alice was there. She always gave off this air like she knew what she was doing, which was exactly the opposite of how I felt.

Eventually, we were called into a tiny interview room with a small table and more of the awful plastic chairs. Alice asked if I'd rather she waited outside. I asked, in a small voice which made me feel annoyingly feeble, if she'd mind coming in with me.

A male officer with salt-and-pepper hair and a huge belly heaved himself into the chair opposite us. He introduced himself as Detective Constable Willis and explained he would be taking down details in order to file a crime report.

I gulped. There was no going back now. Doubts began to resurface. Perhaps it had been a mistake to come here. Alice gave my hand a brief, reassuring squeeze. I took a deep breath and told DC Willis what I knew.

'And this "Spencer", do you know his surname?' DC Willis asked.

'No. Sorry.'

'How long have you known him?'

'Since I started college, last month.'

'So, you agreed to go to the house of a man whose full name you didn't know on a relatively brief acquaintance?' DC Willis was stern now and I felt stupid and small.

'Well, it wasn't actually him that asked me. It was his girlfriend, Sophia.'

'And do you know her surname?'

'Errrr. No.'

DC Willis sighed impatiently.

'OK. And this potential spiking happened last night, you say?'

'Yes.' My voice was coming out squeaky.

'And were you wearing the same clothes you have on at the moment?'

'No. This is my work uniform.'

'What were you wearing last night?'

'What does that have to do with anything?' Alice suddenly interjected, loudly, which made me jump slightly.

'Miss, I'm going to have to ask you to calm down,' DC Willis responded, barely looking in her direction.

'Calm down? As an impartial observer I can clearly see where your line of questioning is heading. You have in front of you a young woman who may very well have been a victim of a serious crime. Yet you seem more concerned with trying to blame her decision-making and sartorial choices than actually investigating it.'

She was leaning forward now, forcing DC Willis to look her in the eye. I'd never heard her speak like that before. It was brilliant, like something out of *Ally McBeal.* I wanted to cheer, but it was like I was paralysed. I could hear ringing in my ears.

'One more word from you, miss, and I shall arrest you for verbally abusing a police officer.' DC Willis was on his feet now, so he towered over her. 'In fact, you are obstructing this interview, so I'm going to have to ask that you step outside.'

'What?'

'STEP. OUTSIDE. MISS.' DC Willis was menacing now and Alice stood reluctantly. She put a hand on my shoulder.

'Will you be OK?'

'She will be fine,' DC Willis responded, before I had a chance to open my mouth.

Once Alice was gone, DC Willis asked, 'What is the nature of your relationship with the young woman who just left, please?'

I was so flustered, I didn't hear him properly. 'Sorry?'

DC Willis rolled his eyes. 'OK, let's start with an easier question. What is her name?' He nodded towards the door behind me.

'Alice.'

'Surname?'

'I don't know.'

'Right.' He snapped his notebook shut. 'Well, since you don't seem prepared to co-operate with the interview and we don't have any details or evidence to go on, I'm afraid we can't take this any further. Have a good day, miss.'

And with that, DC Willis strolled out of the room.

I was stunned. What had just happened? I couldn't make sense of it at all. I felt like I'd done something wrong but I genuinely didn't know what it was. I stood on shaking legs and walked back out into the waiting area, where Alice was pacing up and down, looking agitated. When she saw me, she rushed over and gave me a hug.

'How did it go?' she asked.

'Can we just leave?' I pleaded, suddenly feeling an overwhelming urge to distance myself from the scene of my humiliation.

Once we were outside and had been walking for a few minutes she said, 'I'm sorry.'

'What for?'

'Making you do that. I didn't think they'd be so unhelpful.'

'You weren't to know,' I replied mildly.

She made a kind of annoyed whistling sound. 'I'm a member of the feminist society at my university, you know.'

'Oh, yeah?'

She burst out laughing. 'Could you sound any less interested and enthusiastic?'

'Sorry. My mam said feminists don't shave their legs and burn their bras and for some reason it stuck in my head,' I replied, thinking about how Mam had given me that particular lecture when I'd started repeating Wyn's diatribes about patriarchy.

'OK, it's not how you're imagining it. It's a group of really cool woman and we mostly rant about gender inequality for a bit, swear an oath of allegiance to Alanis Morissette, then drink cider and dance to angry rock.'

'That does sound quite good,' I conceded.

'Anyway, you hear stories all the time about how police aren't interested in helping vulnerable women. I just . . . it's not that I didn't believe them. Of course I did. It's just always the sort of thing you think will happen to someone else, you know?'

I nodded.

'I suppose I wasn't very helpful on the information front,' I said. 'I couldn't even tell him your surname.'

'Well, that isn't really relevant to what happened is it? It's Cox, by the way. And before you say anything, yes, I know there is a deep irony in being a lesbian whose name sounds like "cocks".'

'Thought never crossed my mind,' I replied, my mouth twitching.

'You can laugh,' Alice said with a sigh. 'Everyone does.'

I caved and let out a big belly laugh. It felt really good, like I'd been underwater for ages and had finally broken the surface.

'Seriously, though,' Alice said, after a beat. 'I can bring up your experience with that police officer next time we have a society meeting. We could, I dunno, try and raise awareness or something?'

'I think I just want to leave it,' I said, suddenly so very weary. 'Try and put it behind me. Move on.'

'OK. Well, the offer's there.'

'Thank you.' But I knew, even as I said it, that I wasn't going to be sticking my neck out again.

I felt a bit embarrassed . . . I couldn't work out whether it was because Alice had seen how pathetic I'd been in front of DC Willis, or because I'd dragged her with me to this giant waste of time. Either way, it was like I'd let my new big sister down.

When I sank, at last, into my little single bed at Wyn's, I fell asleep almost as soon as my head hit the pillow.

I dreamt I was back in Spencer's basement. The room was spinning around me. It was far too hot and I was struggling to breathe.

I was crushed between bodies on the dance floor and I wanted to run away, but it was as though I was glued to the spot. When I tried to speak, instead of words, fountains of vomit came out of my mouth and splashed onto the floor. The faces spinning around me pointed and laughed.

Then Spencer grabbed me. He was yelling at me, but it wasn't his voice, it was DC Willis's. 'You're a silly little girl and you deserve everything you get!' he said, dragging me across the floor. I was trying to break free, but I couldn't make my body move.

Then, suddenly, Darsh was there. Rhys was now standing where Spencer had been, wearing a navy uniform and ludicrously large policeman's hat. Darsh drew breath and roared into Rhys's face, so loudly and violently that his whole body heaved with the effort. I began roaring with Darsh, the sound of all the pain and confusion I was feeling but couldn't articulate. With each roar, Rhys shrank smaller and smaller until he was so tiny I couldn't see him any more.

Then I was in Darsh's bed and he was lying next to me, stroking my hair, telling me I was all right. It was so soothing.

But then his voice changed, became higher. The dream began to fade. Darsh was slipping away from me. I tried to hold onto him but I was being pulled from my sleep.

I opened my eyes and realised it was Wyn who was stroking my hair, repeating over and over again, 'You're all right, Cerys. It's OK,'

'Huh?' I mumbled, groggily.

'Ah, there you are, darling,' Wyn whispered. 'I didn't want to wake you suddenly – I read somewhere you're not supposed to do that – but you were having a nightmare. You were screaming in your sleep.'

'Was I?'

'Look at you, you're covered in sweat. Do you want me to change your bed linen?'

I felt about five years old. I thought about saying 'no', that I'd change my sheets myself, but found I didn't have the strength. I just nodded.

'OK, my darling. Go and make yourself a hot drink, or have a wash if you want, and it'll be done in five minutes.'

I winced as I unstuck myself from the clammy bed clothes. I went into the bathroom and wiped the sweat off myself with a flannel. I put on a fresh nightie and then I sat next to the kitchen window clutching a mug of tea.

Wyn stuck her head around the door. 'All done, sweetie. I'm going back to bed now.'

'Thanks,' I replied. 'I'm going to stay here for a bit.'

She nodded, before padding away.

I sat there for hours, long after my tea had become cold, looking at the moon, trying to make sense of everything.

CHAPTER 15

By Monday, I had a plan. I was going to ignore Spencer, Sophia, etc; try to forget Friday ever happened and really focus on my studies. I would simply pretend they didn't exist and fill my mind with arty thoughts.

Unfortunately, my brilliant plan didn't work as quickly as I'd have liked. Sophia insisted on whispering and giggling while looking in my direction in a really obvious way whenever she was nearby. I was sure everyone now knew what had happened at the party. Or her version of it, anyway.

I was hot all the time, like there was a fire burning inside me. Sometimes it felt like humiliation. Other times it felt like anger. I was certain that people must be able to feel it radiating out of me, like I was some sort of human furnace.

I escaped at lunch, heading in the vague direction of the Kings Road. I figured this was as good a time as any to take up Wyn's idea to go on a Bowie/Bolan pilgrimage. It wasn't like I had anything else to fill my lunch hour with.

After I'd been walking for a few minutes, I passed a make-up shop with an amazing window display. It made me do a double take. It was one of those that only stocked one brand

and even a mascara cost something ridiculous like £30. I'd always been too intimidated to go into one of their branches, even though I loved make-up. I usually bought bargain ranges from the chemist. If you applied the products professionally, like they told you to on the beauty pages of *Adept*, they still looked good.

I gazed at the new range of glittery eyeshadows in the window and sighed. They were gorgeous – under-the-sea type shimmery colours, including a really vibrant silver which reminded me of Britney's look in the video for 'Stronger'. I could rock that look, I knew it, but these would be so beyond my budget.

My eye was caught by a hand swiping one of the palettes. Then the hand and the palette disappeared into the pocket of a coat. The person had their back to me. They were obviously watching the shop assistants to make sure they weren't caught stealing. Yet even from behind, there was something really familiar about them.

The thief turned to leave and my brain finally caught up with my instincts. It was Sophia. It was unmistakably her, but that made no sense. She was loaded. Why would she need to shoplift? She emerged from the doorway of the shop. There wasn't time to hide. She saw me standing there and it must have been obvious what I had seen.

For a moment, we just stood and stared at each other, frozen to the spot. Then I marched past her without a word. I wasn't going to say anything until I could work out the best way to handle this. I was feeling so many different things. A bit smug?

Maybe. Turned out Sophia wasn't so much better than the rest of us, after all. Scared? Definitely. This was only going to make her hate me more. Hopeful? Perhaps. I could use this knowledge as leverage. Threaten to tell if she didn't stop being such a bitch all the time . . .

I didn't really know where I was going. I was just walking and thinking about what I'd seen in the window. My phone beeped from somewhere at the bottom of my bag. I tried to put my hand in and grab it as I was walking, but it kept sliding out of my grasp.

I knew better by now than to risk stopping to look for it on the pavement. London pedestrians hated nothing more than an obstacle. I saw a bar that hadn't yet opened and ducked into the space between its doorway and the pavement to rummage.

My nose was in my bag when I felt a body slam into me, pinning me against the glass door. I was so shocked and winded by the force of it, it took me a while to do anything but stand there with my head down, trying to catch my breath. I looked at the shoes that were a few inches from my own. UGG boots. The real deal, not the cheap rip-offs I had in my bedroom. And immaculate, despite their beigeness. They could only belong to one person.

'Sophia,' I gasped. 'What are you—?'

Before I could finish my sentence, she'd slapped me so hard it stung. Then she grabbed my face with one hand. Her square, acrylic nails were digging painfully into my cheeks. Her nose was almost touching mine.

'You didn't see anything, do you understand?' she spat.

I hated how frightened I felt. I could hear my teeth chattering inside my skull where I was shaking so violently. When I spoke, my voice sounded unnaturally high, like a child's.

'OK.'

'And stay away from Spencer, too. He's mine.'

'I have no interest in Spencer! You have to believe me . . .' I pleaded.

'You haaaave to beeeelieve meeee!' Sophia mocked both my accent and the squeaky register of my voice. 'Listen, bitch. I invited you out with us because Spencer said we had to start being nice to you. We felt sorry for you. Then you turn up looking like a whore, flirt with my boyfriend, get completely paralytic and fall down the stairs. Guess that's the thanks I get for trying to be nice.'

'I wasn't flirting! He—'

'We all saw you! Draped all over him! Stop lying!' She was screaming now, her eyes wild and wide. 'Just stay away from us, yeah?' It was the first time I'd heard her say 'yeah' rather than 'yah'. Her accent slipped when she was angry. Pausing only to give me a long, lingering look of disgust, as though I was a particularly stinky piece of dog crap, she spun on her heel and marched away.

I sank down, hugging myself and trembling. There was a sharp tapping on the glass just above my head, which made me jump.

'Excuse me!' said an irritated looking man from inside the bar. 'You can't be loitering here. Shoo!' He made a waving gesture with his hands.

I launched myself back onto the pavement and started to run. My vision was blurry with tears. I kept bumping into people, mumbling 'sorry' and continuing to sprint on, just glimpsing snatches of their coats and hearing their tuts of annoyance as I passed them.

I had no idea where I was going until I got there. Then, all of a sudden, I knew this was where I had been headed all along. The whole thing about Bowie and skip diving had been the excuse I'd told myself to allow me to travel in this direction.

I was outside his block of flats.

I looked up at where I thought his balcony was, wondering if he was home. I remembered his flat number – 604. I could ring his bell. But what would I say? 'It felt like a giant magnet pulled me here and I just had to see you?' That was the truth. But would he get it? Probably not.

I turned to walk away. Then turned back again. I repeated this so many times I must have looked like I was doing some sort of bizarre solo hokey-cokey. I was glad the street was relatively empty.

After a while, I decided if I didn't ring the bell I'd be stuck whirling around for ever. I pressed and waited.

'Hello?'

I gasped. I hadn't thought about what I'd say if he was in. I knew I should run away. He'd never guess it was me. But I felt as though I was glued to the spot.

'Hello?' he said again.

'Darsh?' I asked. I heard my voice wobble.

'Yes. Who is this?'

'It's . . . it's Cerys.' Before I could say anything else, I burst into tears. I was heaving with great big sobs. I kept telling myself I should try and pull it together, but I just didn't seem to be able to. The more I tried to swallow back my tears, the more they forced their way through.

'Cerys!' Darsh was jogging out of the main entrance to his building, towards the huge wrought iron gates I was standing behind. He stopped just before he reached the gates and looked out at me from between the bars. 'Are you OK?' he asked.

I shook my head, not quite looking at him. I could feel him staring at me. He must be working out what he should do. I couldn't blame him, really. Two out of the four times we'd met I'd been sobbing like this. He probably thought I was some sort of emotional wreck.

Eventually, he pressed the button in the bushes and, with agonising slowness, the gates began to open.

There was no barrier between us now and, acting on pure instinct, I ran towards him and flung my arms around his waist. I buried my head into his T-shirt, inhaling his distinctive scent. I immediately felt better. Something about being near him had the instant effect of calming me down.

For a few seconds, he didn't move. Then, very slowly and cautiously, he wrapped his arms around my shoulders, resting his chin on the top of my head.

I felt his body relax and then he tensed up again. 'Come on,' he said. 'We can't stand around in the driveway. You had better come in.'

As we walked towards the building, he reached out and

grabbed my hand. It was weird. I hadn't expected him to do it, but when he did, it felt like the most natural thing in the world. It was like there were sparks travelling up and down my arm from where our hands were touching.

I risked glancing up at him and thought maybe he was thinking the same thing.

CHAPTER 16

It was dark by the time I left Darsh's flat. I didn't really understand where the time had gone. One moment he was offering me a cup of his milk-less tea, the next I looked out of the window and it was dark.

Nothing really happened. Well, nothing of a more than PG nature. I just sat on his sofa, drinking tea and telling him stuff.

Something about him made me feel so comfortable. He never seemed like he was judging me. He just nodded and made 'mmm-hmm' sounds in all the right places, emitting warmth like a human radiator. Every now and then, he'd ask a question.

First, he asked me why I seemed so freaked out when I turned up at his gate. I told him about Sophia. What I'd seen her doing in the make-up shop. What had been going on at college. That last Friday hadn't been an isolated incident. How it was becoming really hard to concentrate in class because she kept finding different ways to torture me, and her friends copied her. I told him that I didn't understand why they were targeting me. I'd never done anything to them.

'I know why,' Darsh said.

'Why?'

'They're jealous.'

I laughed. 'That's like something my mam would say.'

'She's obviously a very wise woman.'

'What is there to be jealous of though? Sophia is rich, popular, gorgeous.' I said, thinking about how, compared to Sophia and her friends, everything about me felt cheap and fake. Like I was the human equivalent off a knock-off handbag.

'You have something she never will.'

'What?'

He stared at me for a moment, probably trying to work out if I was fishing.

'I can't describe it,' he said eventually. 'There's just . . . something about you.'

I didn't know what he meant, but I also believed him. I tucked the moment away in the special place in my memories, promising myself I'd replay it if ever I doubted myself again.

I knew I should probably stop there, move the conversation on to something else. But it was as though a dam had burst and now all my feelings were coming out of my mouth like a tidal wave.

I told him about why I'd come to London from Wales. How I'd built London up in my head as the place that would feel like home. How I'd been expecting it to be glitzy and glamorous and how so far all I'd felt was confused, isolated and terrified. The worst and most unexpected thing of all? How I sometimes felt bored.

Finally, I told him about Rhys. How I'd thought I loved him. How I did, in a way. But it wasn't enough. That he'd become like a brother to me. Part of me just wanted to get it off my chest. The other part really wanted Darsh to know I was single.

'I know what you mean,' he replied, surprising me.

'Huh?' I raised my eyebrows, gesturing for him to go on.

'Where I am from, they like to arrange marriages.'

'Eurgh,' I replied, imagining the sort of pathetic specimen Mam would probably think was a suitable partner for me. Then I quickly checked myself. Was I was being insensitive? 'I mean, I'm sure it works out well for some people . . . It's just, for me, I can't think of anything worse.'

'It makes perfect sense, in a way,' he went on, his eyebrows knitting together like he was trying to do really difficult maths. He looked so cute when he pulled that expression. I had to restrain myself from leaping on him. 'Love is such a powerful emotion. It can blind you to a person's flaws . . .' He was looking directly at me as he said this, which made me wonder who he was talking about and what he thought my flaws were. 'But I just can't imagine saying vows to someone I wasn't in love with. Sharing a house with them. Having children with them. I think it would feel like a lie.'

'Yes,' I breathed. 'That's exactly how I felt with Rhys. I knew logically he was the sort of boy I should be dating. But the whole time I was with him felt like I was acting in a play.'

Darsh nodded. 'So much of life is just going through the motions. Doing what is expected of us. That's what drew me to art,' he said, smiling now. 'It reflects the truth in an uncompromising form. It's a way of expressing all the emotions that society thinks are too ugly or inconvenient to be voiced.'

I'd never thought of art in that way before. I grinned, realising I could quite happily listen to him carry on talking about art for ever. 'I can see why you give lectures.'

'Well, it's only a few.' He shrugged. 'This is really more of a . . . gap year situation, that I'm in.'

I wanted to ask him how he could afford such a swanky flat if he was on a gap year, but worried it might be a rude question, so I just nodded and smiled.

'And I know the stereotype of people with too much money and time wanting to "find themselves" when they go on a gap year,' he continued. I giggled, rolling my eyes. 'But, on the other hand, isn't that what we all want? Isn't that exactly why you came to London?'

'Hmmm. Maybe. No, you know what? It was actually the opposite. I've never felt like I don't know who I am. Just that I was in the wrong place. I needed to get to the place where I belonged. Am I making any sense?'

He nodded, looking at me as though I was one of those Magic Eye puzzles I used to have as a kid. I liked being so fascinating to him. It made me feel exotic and special.

'Do you think . . .' Again, he stopped himself.

'Please, say what you were going to say,' I begged, putting my hand on his arm. I felt the tingles again at our touch.

I held my breath, praying that he would finish his sentence. I hated the idea that he felt like he had to watch what he said around me. I wanted to know whatever was truly on his mind. In fact, if I was being honest, I wanted to burrow *into* his mind and set up camp there, like a little brain rabbit.

He sighed impatiently, but I got the impression he was more cross with himself than with me. 'Do you think that it's not actually places which are our homes, but people?'

'I hadn't thought of it like that before. But now you say it . . . yes.'

Time seemed to stand still. I wondered if he was going to kiss me. I wished so hard that he would.

But he didn't. Instead he stood up abruptly and said, 'It's getting late.'

'FUCK!' I shouted, registering the inky night sky beyond the French window.

Everything was a blur of grabbing my jacket and phone and an awkward hugged goodbye. Then, before I knew it, I was out on the street again, feeling the shock of the cold evening air on my face, wondering what the hell just happened.

Wyn was, predictably, furious when I got in at just past 10 p.m. All her cool auntie traits were slowly being peeled away, like the layers of an onion. At her core she was actually more like Mam than she'd ever admit.

'We have had this discussion, Cerys!' she said, before she even said hello to me, wearily putting her fingers to her temples.

I walked straight past her and into my tiny room. I wanted to slam the door, but the clothes curtain was in the way, so I settled for throwing myself on the bed and huffing instead. I didn't know why I was so furious.

After a few moments, Wyn came in. She perched one half of

her bum on the bed. I twisted away from her so I was looking at the wall.

'You've always been so grown-up for your age, darling,' Wyn said, her voice much gentler, now. 'But you have to understand that you're still a minor, which means I'm responsible for you. You're only sixteen . . .'

'Nearly seventeen!' I objected. It was ironically quite a childish thing to say.

'Yes, I know. But even so. Perhaps you need more guidance than I'm giving you.' She muttered the last part, as though she was talking to herself. A silence hung in the air. For the first time ever, it was awkward between us. I looked at my feet while I tried to think of something to say.

'Darling,' Wyn suddenly broke the silence. 'I have to ask you something.'

I nodded once, grumpily.

'The reason you keep coming back late—'

'I don't *keep* coming back late!' I interjected, my voice high and screechy. 'It's happened twice!'

I didn't like this version of me – the whiny one. It was usually only Mam that brought it out in me. I wanted Wyn to think I was mature and complex. Yet I couldn't seem to help myself.

'Fine.' Wyn sighed. 'The reason you have been late back twice . . . Is it because you are seeing someone?'

'No,' I retorted and then immediately wondered whether it was technically true.

'It's just, I know you have broken up with Rhys.'

'What? How do you know that?'

'Delia told me.' Wyn at least had the decency to look a bit guilty as she said this.

'So, hang on, you and Mam have been talking about me behind my back?'

'Not exactly. She rings sometimes, to ask how you are getting on. It's only natural. She is your mother after all, darling.'

'Sounds like spying to me. Anyway, how come Mam knows about me and Rhys?'

'He went around to the farmhouse. Was in quite the state, apparently. Heartbroken, is how Delia described it.'

I didn't know how to feel about this at all. On the one hand, it was horrible to think of Rhys upset. I did still care about him, even if he had been a total bastard. On the other, there was something that felt wrong about him going to Mam and Da's to get his side of the story across, before I'd had the chance. Like he was trying to turn my parents against me.

'And you think the only reason I could have broken up with Rhys is because I've found someone else?' I was stalling. Something told me it wouldn't be a good idea to tell Wyn about Darsh. At least not yet.

'I didn't say that.'

Another silence, during which I heard the distance sound of a Hoover as one of Wyn's upstairs neighbours clattered about doing housework.

'Have you had the safe sex talk, darling?' Wyn said this quickly, as though it was just as excruciating for her to say as it was for me to hear.

Mam would rather have stapled her eyelids to a table than

talk to me about sex. In Year 9, we'd had to watch a video of cartoon sperms fertilising an egg as a stern voiceover told us the only way to completely avoid this was to "abstain". When the video finished our teacher had reminded us that abstaining meant AVOIDING SEX ALTOGETHER and then asked us if we had any questions (in a way that made it really obvious she hoped we didn't). It wasn't exactly a useful class, but we were all too embarrassed to put our hand up to ask anything. The rest I'd picked up from the magazines I read.

I just said, 'Of course.'

'Well, good.' Wyn stood up. 'And if you need to talk to me about anything, I am here. Remember that.'

'Thanks.' I looked at her for the first time since she'd come in and all my anger left my body in an instant, like I was a balloon that had been popped with a pin.

She was still my Auntie Wyn. The woman who had first inspired my love of fashion by turning up at the farmhouse for Christmas wearing fabulous outfits. The person who'd first put the idea of London in my head by telling me stories about her adventures in that far off, magical place. Who'd made me feel grown-up and sophisticated at thirteen by letting me have half a glass of wine, topped up with lemonade, with dinner. Whose flat had always felt like my sanctuary.

Impulsively, I stood up too and gave her a hug. Maybe everything was going to be OK.

CHAPTER 17

I tried putting 'That Don't Impress Me Much' by Shania Twain on my CD Walkman. Usually, it was the song I played to make me feel all sassy and confident, but it didn't work this time for some reason. After the track ended, I just felt numb.

I read in *Adept* once that in order to feel confident you have to repeat a 'mantra' to yourself. Something like, 'I am a strong, powerful woman'. If you say it enough, apparently, you start to really believe it.

I looked at myself in the mirror. Black trousers. One of those jumpers which looks like you're wearing a shirt underneath but actually just has cuffs and the hem of a shirt stitched onto it. Ironed hair. I looked chic and put together. Kind of like Rachel Green, actually, but after she quit being a waitress and gets the job in fashion.

'I am a strong, powerful woman,' I said to my reflection. The me in the mirror looked back uncertainly.

'I AM A STRONG POWERFUL WOMAN!' I repeated, louder this time.

'What, darling?' Wyn's voice floated down the corridor from the kitchen. She was headed into her office today, so I knew she'd be drinking her first cup of tea and smoking out of the window.

'Nothing!' I yelled back, feeling stupid.

I sighed, exasperated. I'd never had an issue with confidence before. Back in Wales, it was just something I had, in the same way I had grey eyes or blonde hair. I never noticed how invincible I used to feel until I didn't any more.

I searched my memory pocket, where all the compliments were stored. Rhys telling me I was 'in the top two per cent of women in the world, beauty-wise'. That time I was shopping with my friends in Carmarthen and a woman told me I walked like a supermodel. Wyn saying how I'd always been grown-up. Then, of course, there was Darsh.

Darsh telling me the bullies were jealous of me. That I had something. Something so special he – one of the most articulate people I'd ever met – couldn't quite define it. That memory was the one that did the trick. The warm glow of his words coated my insides, like syrup. I felt stronger, more powerful than I had just seconds before. Darsh was my mantra.

I snatched up my bag and did my best Rachel-Green-after-she-gets-her-dream-job strut out of the door.

I've never walked into a room and had everyone immediately fall silent, before.

The moment I crossed the threshold into my first class of the day, still wearing Darsh's opinion of me like a suit of armour, everyone just stopped talking. All in the same second.

'What?' I said, as twenty pairs of eyes stared at me with

distaste. I looked down at my shoes to see if there was a piece of toilet paper trailing from them, simultaneously running my finger underneath my nose in case I had a bogey. Even as I did this, it occurred to me that neither of those things was enough to provoke the reaction I'd just got.

No one was answering me. They all just continued to gawp at me like fishes. The silence was deafening.

Finally, someone moved. It was Sophia, who stood up and began to giggle at the same time. When she spoke, her voice was breathy and saccharine sweet.

'I think maybe you'd better go into the hall,' she said. 'There's something there you'll probably want to see.'

I didn't need telling twice. As I pegged it out of the room, I could just about make out Sophia saying in her normal voice, 'I mean, I'm sure she already knows. She probably did it herself. Attention seeker.'

I could hear thundering in my ears as I ran down empty corridors which seemed to stretch for miles. I tucked my chin into my chest, trying to contain my panic. Suddenly, I headbutted something firm and warm.

'Cerys.' I felt a hand on each of my shoulders. I dared myself to look up, already knowing it was him.

Even in my flustered state, my first thought was to wonder what I looked like to Darsh, in that moment. Was my expression as wild as the feelings inside me? Did I look mad? Was my hair, which I'd spent at least thirty minutes meticulously straightening that morning, now messy? I admitted to myself, right then, that part of the extra care I'd taken getting ready had been inspired by the hope of running into him today. I just hadn't realised how literally that would happen. I wished there was a mirror nearby so I could check myself.

'Are you OK?' he asked.

I didn't know how to answer that question, so I just shook my head.

'Have you been into the hall?' Again, I shook my head. I didn't seem to be able to tear my eyes away from his, or blink.

I heard the distant clip-clop of shoes on the polished floor and Darsh quickly dropped his arms so we were no longer touching. He turned to face whoever it was walking towards us. As he came into view, I recognised him as the principal. He'd done a speech welcoming us on our first day of college. He was a short round man with greying hair. He had an imposing sort of vibe about him, like a perma-grumpy Santa Claus.

'Ms Williams,' he said in a serious tone. 'I am glad Mr Nadeem here managed to locate you. Would you follow me, please?'

Meekly, I did. I could sense Darsh behind me and couldn't decide whether it was better or worse that he would be there to witness whatever would follow.

When we reached the hall, I could see a projector had been set up close to the entrance, pointed at the back wall. I followed the trail of light. At first, my eyes could only take in small parts of the enormous image. An elbow here. The spilt contents of a handbag there. When it eventually dawned on me what I was looking at, I gasped.

It was me, dressed in the outfit I'd been wearing the night of

Spencer's house party. I was sprawled out on the pavement, one leg sticking out at a strange angle. My eyes were half closed. My skirt had ridden up, revealing my knickers.

I remembered the moment it had been taken. How sick and dizzy I had felt. How confused I was, wondering why no one was helping me get up. How they'd laughed at me instead. Then, the flash.

'Ms Williams,' the principal's voice interrupted my thoughts. 'Are you able to tell us anything about how this image came to be projected on our wall?'

I wanted to look away, but couldn't seem to tear my eyes from the photo. I tried to speak, but there were no coherent words. Nothing I could say that would even go halfway to answering the principal's question. I heard him sigh, then say, 'Switch it off, please.' There was a click and then the picture disappeared, leaving us cloaked in artificial darkness.

'Please come to my office at eleven o'clock and be prepared to tell me everything you know about how this happened.' I was still too stunned to reply. The principal clip-clopped out of the room.

It was Darsh who broke the silence. I'd almost forgotten he was standing behind me and jumped slightly at the sound of his voice.

'Tell me what you're thinking, Cerys.'

'I'm . . . I'm not thinking anything,' I replied. Even as I said it, I realised that wasn't quite the case. It was less that I had a lack of thoughts and more that too many were crowding my brain for me to be able to focus on a single one.

Darsh waited patiently. After a moment I said, 'I suppose I'm wondering . . . why? Why would someone do this to me? All I've ever done since I arrived here is try to fit in. I've never hurt anyone. How could somebody hate me this much?'

He didn't reply, just checked to make sure no one could see us before wrapping his arms around me. I leant back into the embrace. It was like coming up for air. Whatever else I had to face today, there was at least this moment.

CHAPTER 18

Looking back, I probably should have guessed that the whole photo incident would have ended up being seen as my fault. The principal had seemed cross with me in the hall. At the time, I'd been too distracted to notice. But when I walked into his office it was obvious he was furious . . .

I got the impression he didn't believe me when I told him I didn't know exactly who had taken the photo, or who had projected it onto the wall. He even seemed sceptical when I said I hadn't posed for it. As though anyone would choose to make themselves look that bad. He asked if I thought it was 'art' or even vaguely amusing and then just grunted when I told him I did not. I'm sure he thought I was deliberately holding stuff back.

I was suspended for a week for displaying artwork without permission and causing disruption. I knew it was unfair, but arguing would only make the situation worse. Everything I said seemed the make the principal more irritated with me. And I couldn't mention Sophia or Spencer without having definitive proof. Not unless I wanted to be slammed into a door again. Or worse.

Wyn insisted that I shouldn't sit around feeling sorry for myself. 'It'll give you wrinkles, darling.' But I think it was actually the prospect of being cooped up with another human, 24/7, in her custom-designed cocoon that filled her with horror.

She instructed me to get my 'pert little bottom' down to Sunny Side Up and enquire about extra shifts.

I had a feeling that if I was alone with my thoughts for too long, I might spontaneously combust with the injustice of everything. Part of me couldn't believe I'd ended up here, with everything being seen as my fault and no way to prove otherwise. I tried to be mature. To push the thoughts away. I told myself life was unfair and I had to get used to it. That this was what being an adult was.

When I turned up at Sunny Side, I was relieved to see it was Alice who was behind the counter. I'd deliberately picked the lull-time between the breakfast and lunch rushes. The café was empty, aside from a slightly shifty looking guy wearing a long beige anorak, who was nursing a cup of tea in the corner.

Alice was sat on a high stool behind the gleaming glass display of cakes and pastries, reading a massive text book. She grinned and jumped down when she saw me, running around to give me a hug. I explained that I had a bit of extra free time that week and asked if there were any shifts going.

'I don't think so, hun,' she said. 'I can double-check later on, though.'

'OK, thanks anyway,' I replied, trying not to look as dejected as I felt. 'See you soon, I guess.'

'Hey!' Alice exclaimed, as I was turning to leave. 'A bunch

of us are going out this Friday – we're meeting outside here at seven then heading to Hammersmith. Do you want to join? I know you don't really know the whole gang, but it'll be fun, I promise.' She winked, which made me wish I had the ability to wink with her confidence. I'd tried winking in front of a mirror once and just looked like I had something in my eye.

I thought about saying no. Last time I'd tried to party, bad things had happened and I'd ended up in a mess. But then I thought it was bound to be different this time, when I had a big sister with me. Looking out for me.

'Love to,' I said. 'Count me in.'

In the days after, I distracted myself from the grimness of my reality – being suspended during my first term at college; everyone having seen a massive picture of me sprawled out in an embarrassing drunken stupor; not knowing what Sophia was planning next; the fact I hadn't heard anything from Darsh even though I'd given him my number – by focussing on going out with Alice. I imagined Alice and her friends, dancing and drinking in Hammersmith. I imagined myself with them, laughing along with their conversations. I tried to bring the image to life, but, below our heads, we were just blurry shapes. I couldn't picture what any of us were wearing.

I'd only ever seen Alice in our work uniform of dark trousers and an apron with a massive fried egg stitched onto it. I didn't know anything about her style. *Adept* had an article on what 'London's young glitterati' were wearing . . . Maybe if I tried to copy that?

With hours to go before I was due to meet them, I stood contemplating the wardrobe-curtain for the thousandth time. I was just seeing if there was anything I could fashion into a handkerchief top, when my phone beeped. I wondered who it could be. Rhys was still giving me the silent treatment, which was fine by me. The few friends I had back in Wales had long ago stopped checking in. Probably they believed his version of events. I couldn't say I was surprised. They were his friends to begin with.

I snuffled around trying to find my phone, eventually locating it in one of my shoes.

Just checking to see how you are.
Darsh x

My heart started to thunder at the sight of his name. When it fully registered that he'd put a kiss at the end of his message I felt like I might pass out. I thought about waiting before I replied. There was something slightly sad about jumping straight on my phone when it made a noise. I didn't want Darsh to think I was just sitting around, doing nothing (even though that's exactly what I was doing). Although, what if when I did reply he was busy doing something else and didn't see it? The agony of waiting for him to respond would be too much. It was only about ten seconds before the urge to send something back became too strong to ignore.

Am OK thank you.

I typed, using the same formal tone as him, spelling out my words in full.

Was suspended for a week. Annoying but am going out tonight with friends from work x

A couple of seconds later, my phone began to ring. His number flashed up on the screen. I took a deep breath. Considered letting it ring out. Then I told myself I was being stupid. There was no reason to be this nervous and I absolutely had to know what he was calling to say. I pressed the green button.

'Hello?'

'Hi, Cerys. I'm glad you're OK. But . . . are you sure it's a good idea to go out tonight?'

'How do you mean?'

'Well . . . what happened to you last time you accepted an invitation from people you thought were friends?'

It was a rhetorical question. We both knew what had happened. I'd been utterly humiliated. Twice, now. It had all been a trick. Alice didn't seem like the sort of person who would do something like that, but all of a sudden, I didn't trust my own judgment.

'I can't just sit indoors for the rest of my life,' I said huffily.

'Of course not.' Darsh sounded hurt and I felt bad for snapping at him. 'That's not what I'm suggesting. I'm just worried about you, is all.'

'You're worried about me?'

'Yes.'

'Why?'

'You know why.'

'No, I don't. Tell me.' I wanted to hear him say it. I wanted confirmation that everything I'd been feeling wasn't one-sided.

'I like you, Cerys.' There was something about how he said my name, in his deep voice with his slight accent, that made me feel like I was melting.

'I like you too.' My grin was so wide my cheeks hurt.

There was a beat of silence, but I could somehow tell that he was smiling as well.

'Listen, it is the start of Diwali. Would you like to come and celebrate with me?'

I didn't even have to think about it. We arranged to meet at his flat that evening.

I wanted to text Alice to tell her I wasn't coming out after all. I could have said I had a headache or something, but didn't have her number. We'd never met outside of post-shift dunch before that point. I wondered how she would feel when I didn't show. How long she and the others would wait for me. Whether she would hold it against me and be in a mood the next time I saw her at Sunny Side. A little cloud settled over my head.

Then, as I thought about Darsh, the cloud dispersed as quickly as it came. He liked me too. Maybe he would kiss me, this time. I thought about his intelligent dark eyes, the way his cheeks dimpled when he smiled, the way he smelt. That evening suddenly felt like a long time away . . . Still, there was something delicious about the anticipation of being near him again.

I hugged myself, smiling, before it occurred to me I had a big problem . . .

I had no idea what Diwali was.

CHAPTER 19

'I'm going to the library,' I yelled, more confidently than I felt, shouldering my bag and marching towards the door with determination.

'You're what, darling?' Wyn looked confused.

'Going to the library! There's surely one around here, isn't there?'

'Well, yes, actually. There's a big one on the Broadway. But are you going to . . . read?'

'I do read sometimes!'

Wyn glanced at her copy of *Bridget Jones's Diary*, which she'd lent me the week I'd arrived and could be seen through my bedroom door, where it had been abandoned on the floor.

'Well, OK then, darling. Wrap up warm, won't you? There's a chill in the air.'

Of course, I wasn't actually going there to read. I needed to find out what Diwali was without looking like a tit. I assumed it was one of those things everyone in London knew and if I asked I was basically declaring 'I DO NOT BELONG HERE'. There was only one thing for it: I was going to have to

Ask Jeeves. And in order to do that, I needed a computer with access to the internet.

I'd rather eat my own elbow than admit it, but Wyn had been right to be shocked when I announced I was going to the library. I wasn't exactly a renowned lover of literature.

In fact, I only managed to scrape a C in my English GCSE thanks to Baz Luhrmann. His film made *Romeo and Juliet* a lot less boring, even if our teacher kept warning us that the script cut over two thirds of the original text. It was much easier to understand what old Wills was on about when his words were emitting from the gorgeous mouth of Leonardo DiCaprio.

I just didn't really understand why you'd want to read some old book full of gibberish when there were lovely glossy magazines full of gossip, fashion and relevant advice.

I found the library easily enough and hovered nervously around the entrance wondering what the protocol was. There was a kindly looking woman sitting behind a large desk to my left, seemingly engrossed in sorting books into two cardboard boxes. I decided I'd ask her. I was quickly learning that, as much as London could be quite scary, the advantage of living in such an enormous city was that you very rarely bumped into people you knew by accident. Even if the woman laughed in my face and said, 'What do you MEAN you don't know how to use a public library, you idiot?' I'd never have to see her again.

Fortunately, she didn't. She patiently explained that I'd have to fill in a form to get membership to the library, after which she'd give me a slip of paper that was a token worth fifteen minutes of internet time.

'This is for computer number two,' she said, indicating a machine which a man was currently hunched over. 'When his time is up, you can jump right on it.'

After thanking her, I hovered nearby, slowly meandering up and down shelves stuffed with books, some with yellowing pages and creases in the spines. There was a really distinctive smell that was hard to describe – kind of sweet and musty, but not unpleasant. I quite liked it. I wondered if anyone had ever made a perfume of it.

It was so peaceful and warm in the library that by the time the guy on computer number two stood to leave I felt like I'd gone into a kind of trance. I wandered over to the screen and typed in the code the librarian had given me. Then I clicked on the internet icon.

Of course, I knew how to use the web. I sent emails sometimes. We'd had IT lessons at school. But I hadn't really got into chat rooms the way some of the people in my year had. It's not that I didn't think it sounded like fun. I thought about going on MSN Messenger at one point. But then Rhys had said he didn't think it was a good idea – I'd get chatted up too much by 'random old pervs pretending to be our age', he said. Then I'd just never got around to it.

I fired up Ask Jeeves like we'd been shown in computer science class at school. The cartoon butler popped up – the one we'd been told could answer any question we could think of. I typed *What is Diwali?* into the search bar, then clicked on the red 'ask' button.

Diwali is a religious festival. It celebrates the victory of light over darkness and lasts for five days. Diwali starts on the fifteenth day of the month of Kartika, according to the Hindu calendar, and ends with the Hindu new year. In the Western calendar, it is usually the month of October or November.

So, Darsh was Hindu. Which one was that again? I was really starting to regret not paying more attention in religious studies.

What do Hindus believe?

Hindus believe in samsara, which is reincarnation, and karma, which means for every cause there is an effect. One of the key beliefs in Hinduism is 'atman', which means 'soul'. Hindus believe that all living creatures have a soul. In turn, they also believe we are all part of one supreme soul.

Well, that sounded cool. I loved the idea of reincarnation. I often thought I'd like to come back as a bird. I could fly wherever my wings carried me, never having to explain to anyone where I was going, or ask permission. Bliss.

By the time I'd blinked out of my fantasies about how it might feel to be truly free, soaring through the clouds, detached from all the human rules, I only had five minutes left to ask Jeeves the most important question of all.

What do people wear for Diwali? Search

As I walked down the corridor to the entrance to Darsh's flat, he stepped out of his front door, took one look at me and burst out laughing. I caught sight of my reflection in the surface of a No Smoking sign and had to admit I did look a bit . . . eccentric.

There was some confusion about what colour people were supposed to wear for Diwali when I asked Jeeves, but he'd said black 'acknowledged the auspiciousness of the occasion' so I went with that. Jeeves also told me that it was traditional to wear a saree and that many Hindu women accessorized with a lot of gold jewellery.

I was wearing the closest thing to a saree I could find (an oversized black sequinned kaftan of Wyn's) with pretty much every piece of jewellery I owned. I'd draped one of my necklaces over my head and pinned it in place with kirby grips so the pendant – which was a tear-shaped mood stone – hung just above my eyebrows. Now I was here I couldn't remember exactly why or when, but somehow I'd got it into my head that this was what Hindu people did.

Darsh was wearing a pair of jeans and what looked like a cashmere sweater, just like he did most other days. I stood completely still in the hallway, feeling conflicted. As much as I felt like a complete arse, I'd also made Darsh laugh. His laugh was my favourite sound, his smile the best thing I'd ever seen. It was worth the humiliation. Almost.

Darsh recovered himself and held out a hand, gesturing for me to come towards him.

'I'm sorry,' he said. 'Thank you for making an effort. I do appreciate it. But you didn't have to.'

I shuffled towards him, my cheeks burning. I kept my gaze on his shoes until our toes were practically touching. Then I felt his fingers gently cup my chin. He lifted my head and our eyes met.

The whole day up until this point, I'd done nothing but think about him. Yet for some reason, I wasn't prepared for the impact that actually looking at him would have on me. That face. Those eyes. I actually felt weak at the knees, which I had previously assumed was only something people said in romantic dramas on TV.

'Really,' he murmured. 'Please don't be embarrassed. It's sweet that you did this.' It would have been so easy to kiss him then. I'd only have to have move my head slightly. It felt like he wanted me to. Yet, after my outfit disaster, I didn't want to risk getting another thing wrong. So I just nodded.

He took my hand and led me into his flat. It looked completely different from the last time I'd been here. Then, it had been anonymous and sparse. Now, flickering candles covered every surface and delicious smells were wafting from the kitchen area. My mouth watered.

'So, as you might have guessed, I don't know anything about Diwali,' I said, laughing to cover my earlier embarrassment.

'It's OK,' he replied easily, opening the oven to check on something inside. 'It's my fault really. I forgot to explain.'

He told me to sit and I did, trying to subtly remove the necklace from my head as I went.

'Diwali is a festival of light. We get together to eat with people we . . . value . . .' He tripped over his words here, which made me think he'd been about to say, 'people we love'. I wished he had. 'And usually there are fireworks, but I don't have any of those.'

'When you say "we",' I asked, 'do you mean Hindus?'

'Well, yes, although Sikh and Jain people also celebrate it, and some Muslims too.'

'So, which one are you?' I blurted. As Darsh's brow creased, I panicked that I'd insulted him.

'That's a difficult question to answer. I was raised Hindu. My family are practising. But I don't follow any faith. I am . . . atheist.'

'So, why do you still mark Diwali?' I asked.

'Do you go to church?'

'No.'

'But you celebrate Christmas?'

'OK, good point.'

'For me, it's a chance to eat good food and spend time with family and friends. It's just that I don't have so many of those, here in London. Well, I have an uncle who lives a few miles away, but . . . I thought you might be feeling lonely after what happened and . . . I'd rather spend it with you.'

'Oh.' There was a long silence as I tried to find some appropriate words.

I knew what my heart wanted me to do. It was telling me to say, 'I'm so glad you asked me here tonight, Darsh, because I care about you. I think I might even be falling in love with you. I know it's really soon. We've only known each other five minutes, but somehow I just know it. And I think you might know it too.'

The thing was, I was realising that 'I like you' was a phrase massively open to interpretation. I had thought at the time he meant he liked me in a girlfriend way, the same way I liked him, but he could have meant in a friend way. What if I told Darsh how I felt and he laughed at me and called me a silly little girl? What if he said that he just invited me over because he knew I had no friends and he felt sorry for me? I didn't think I could bear it. I'd have to implode with shame. Or go back to Wales. Both options were equally unappealing.

So, instead I said, 'What are we eating?'

My question did its job – it pierced the tension of the moment. Darsh stood and brushed his hands against his jeans as he strolled back over to the kitchen.

'I made paneer tikka and lentil daal.'

'Great!' I replied brightly, pretending I had understood anything apart from the 'tikka' in that description.

'I hope I got it right. It's been a while since I watched my mother make this dish,' he replied, retrieving food from the oven and bringing over two steaming bowls.

On one side of my bowl were some cubes of something whiteish and solid in a rusty red glaze. On the other was what looked like brown porridge. It didn't look particularly appetizing but it smelt out of this world. Cautiously, I dipped my spoon into the lentils, blew on them and put them in my mouth. Darsh watched me intently.

'OH MY GOD!' I exclaimed.

'What?' He sounded alarmed.

'This is the most delicious thing I've ever tasted!'

He chuckled. 'Phew!' he pretended to wipe his brow and tucked into his own bowl. We chewed in silence for a while.

'If I say so myself, I have done a good job,' said Darsh.

'It's SO GOOD,' I confirmed. 'I never want to eat anything else ever again.'

He laughed again. I loved that I had the power to break his stern exterior 'More?'

This question presented a dilemma. Veronica Bailey said in one of her columns you shouldn't shovel down food in front of a man you fancied, but instead eat in a delicate and alluring way. On the other hand, I wasn't lying when I said it was the best thing I'd ever put in my mouth.

It was like he could read my thoughts. 'You know, where I am from it is considered attractive when a woman has a healthy appetite.'

Wordlessly, I held out my empty bowl to him and he laughed. 'Second helpings coming up.'

The second portion was just as delicious as the first, but my mind was elsewhere. I was thinking about how he'd used the words 'attractive' and 'woman' and wondering whether he was picturing me when he said them. I sat up a little taller, trying to angle my body so I'd look thin and curvy at the same time from where he was sitting.

'You don't have to do that you know, Cerys.'

'What?' I was pretending not to know what he meant. I'd broken the number one rule of being sexy, which is that you should never be seen to be trying.

'You don't have to sit like the models on billboards do. You are beautiful.'

'Am I?'

'I think you know you are. But I also think you don't know what it is that makes you beautiful. It's when you're relaxed. When you forget yourself. When you're not covered in make-up. Like, that time when we saw each other outside the café and you were doing this kind of . . . mime? To remind me of how we'd met before?'

'Oh, god. I remember that! I felt like such a goof.'

'But that's the thing, Cerys. I remember thinking, OK, so, she can be funny. She can laugh at herself. She isn't just an attractive airhead.'

'You thought I was an airhead before?'

'Maybe. It would be easy for someone who looks like you not to have a personality . . . but you have the full package.'

I didn't think it was possible to misinterpret what he was saying any more. He liked me in the girlfriend way.

I stood up, slowly.

He put his bowl on the coffee table, never taking his eyes off me.

I sat on his lap and wrapped my arms around his neck. He was warm and solid. My body slotted into his like we were pieces of a jigsaw.

I felt his hands on my waist. His grip was strong, but I also sensed that he was holding himself back, waiting for me to make another move.

I kissed him.

There were Diwali fireworks, after all.

CHAPTER 20

'Well, he's just a little bit handsome, isn't he?' Wyn trilled, as soon as the door to the office had closed behind us. I hurried her further along the corridor, worried we were still in their earshot.

'What, the principal?'

'No, darling. That other chap. Nadeem, I think it was? Intense eyes. Fabulous hair. He's made me come over all a-quiver. If I was twenty years younger . . .'

'Ewww! Can you stop, please?'

'Oh, come on, darling. You've always enjoyed my little flights of erotic fantasy in the past. Don't spoil my fun now.'

'Yes, well. You're my legal guardian now, which means you're the closest thing I have to a parent, which means the thought of you shagging is officially gross,' I snapped. There was no need to tell her why I really wanted to halt this conversation as quickly as possible – Darsh was mine.

We'd kissed for what felt like hours but was also not long enough, the night of the Diwali dinner. That night, every song lyric I'd ever listened to about passion, the ones that likened it to fire and electricity, made sense. This was the real deal.

I had never known kissing like that. Rhys and I had officially become 'boyfriend and girlfriend' when I was thirteen and he was fifteen. Snogging him had been a nice enough way to pass the time, but I could mostly take or leave it, especially when he moved his tongue round in circles like a washing machine. I'd had the odd kiss with boys before Rhys, but it was mostly experimental, playground stuff, with lots of lots of headbutting and clashes of teeth.

With Darsh, it was as though I could literally feel the air between us crackling. I didn't have time to think about whether our mouths were at the optimum angles, or whether my breath smelt, or where I should put my hands. It just . . . happened.

When our lips were sore from all the kissing, we talked about our plans to keep it all secret. How we'd act around each other at college. He wasn't an official member of staff or anything, but if it got out that we were seeing each other, Darsh thought he would still probably get in trouble.

I couldn't think of anyone I wanted to tell, anyway. After living in a tiny village and every part of my life being public knowledge, it felt good to have something that was just mine. The secret made me feel cocooned somehow, like I was in a constant cwtch.

I smiled to myself as sexy little vignettes from the previous night floated through my mind. The way he had grabbed the kaftan I'd nicked from Wyn and scrunched it up in his hands, pulling me even closer to him. How grown-up and desired that had made me feel. How he had whispered 'you're so beautiful, Cerys' in my ear, his hot breath sending tingles down my spine.

The way we had to keep stopping because he said kissing was enough for now and he had to control himself. How there was part of me that wished he wouldn't . . .

I couldn't wait to see him again that evening.

In the meantime, the principal had called Wyn and me in for a meeting. I was surprised to find Darsh sitting next to him when we walked into the office. It was explained that Darsh, or 'Mr Nadeem' as the principal insisted on calling him, had been witness to some of the 'key events' leading up to my suspension and was therefore present to 'corroborate my version of events'. It was like we were in an episode of *The Bill*, or something.

As the principal explained what had happened to Wyn in a self-important way, she became more and more agitated. Finally, she exploded.

'I think it is outrageous that you have punished Cerys for something which is clearly not her fault.'

'It's OK, Wyn,' I soothed, embarrassed by her outburst.

'It's not OK though, is it?' She dismissed me with an 'I'll deal with you later' type gesture and I gulped. I'd never really seen Wyn this angry before. I had a feeling she could be even scarier if she put her mind to it. Worse than Mam, even. 'I don't suppose any effort has been put into finding the little scrotes actually responsible for exploiting and humiliating my niece?'

'Ms Evans,' the principal boomed, making me jump a little in my chair. 'I can assure you we have taken the incident seriously. All students in the art department were spoken to and we reminded them of the high standards of conduct we expect from them. We also urged anyone with any information to come forward. So far, they have not.'

'Well, I for one am shocked and stunned,' Wyn retorted sarcastically and I saw Darsh quickly hide a smile behind his hand.

'I understand,' the principal continued, as though Wyn hadn't spoken, 'that up until recently Cerys was living in Wales. Perhaps the move to London has been difficult for her? We have various resources available, in case you require extra support.'

'She's fine. We're fine,' Wyn said, standing up and sweeping her vast cloak of a coat off the back of her chair, flinging it around her shoulders. I had to duck to avoid being smacked in the face.

'I think you at least need to have a discussion about how Cerys can dress more appropriately so she doesn't find herself in this situation again,' said the principal.

Wyn, who had been about to sashay out of the room, stopped abruptly and turned to face him. Very quietly, in almost a whisper, she said, 'Excuse me?'

'It is clear from the image which has caused all this . . . *hoopla*, that Cerys was in an extremely vulnerable position. She was both intoxicated and dressed in an very provocative manner. For her safety, it would be prudent if she did neither of these things again.'

Wyn didn't speak for at least three seconds. I looked down at her hand and saw it was clenched into a fist. I glanced at Darsh but saw that he too was staring at Wyn, waiting for the inevitable eruption.

'Do you not think that it would be better for the safety of all the young women in this college if it didn't contain misogynistic bastards who think it's fun to humiliate their female peers?' Wyn was the one booming now. She usually only sounded like this when she'd had a few glasses of wine and wanted to rant about the patriarchy (usually at family gatherings with Mam rolling her eyes extravagantly and saying 'give it a rest will you, Blodwyn' at regular intervals).

The principal rose from his chair now. He and Wyn stared at each other like cowboys in old films do just before a shoot-off. I thought about standing up too but it was like I was frozen in my seat, waiting to see who was going to be first to pull their trigger.

'I can see we are not going to agree on the best way forward, Ms Evans. I suggest a period of monitoring for Cerys and, if further concerns arise, perhaps involving her parents.'

I looked at Wyn, willing her to nip this terrifying idea in the bud. Instead, it was Darsh who spoke.

'I am sorry to say this, Principal Stevens, but I have to say I agree with Ms Evans on this matter. Whilst we cannot endorse the underage drinking' – he shot me a look as he said this and I could feel my heart thundering in my chest – 'Cerys is the wronged party here. Surveilling her further, especially after her suspension, feels like an unnecessary continuation of her punishment.'

For a moment, it felt like I was floating outside of my body watching this weird scene. My secret boyfriend – who knew more about what had really happened that night than anyone else in the room – siding with my oblivious aunt against my weirdly old-fashioned principal. All of them talking about my life, deciding on my future. None of them – apart from the odd glance from Darsh – even looking at me. They were treating me as though I was a naughty child – the very last thing I wanted to be. Especially, it was the last thing I wanted Darsh to see me as. I could feel our new, post-kiss status as equals slipping through my fingers.

'I will behave, I promise,' I found myself saying, even though that wasn't at all what I was thinking. What I was thinking was, *I'm going to actually die from sheer humiliation if this meeting doesn't end soon.*

'Well, I think that's a satisfactory conclusion to this meeting then,' said the principal, returning to his chair.

Thank god. I leapt up and dragged Wyn from the room. It had taken precisely four seconds for her to forget she was angry and start wanging on about how hot Darsh was. It was hard to know which was preferable, to be honest.

'Are you OK, darling? You look as though you have gone into a trance,' Wyn asked as we approached the entrance to college.

I looked at my favourite relative, so statuesque and stylish in her cape and turban, and felt this overwhelming rush of sadness. If circumstances were different – if Darsh was just another student at the college – I'd be dying to tell her all the details of our make-out session. Well, maybe not all of them . . . but I'd definitely tell her we'd snogged and point Darsh out from a distance so I could show off about how fit he was.

But everything had changed now. Wyn wasn't my eccentric,

cool aunt any more. She was the person who got called into disciplinary meetings at the college when I'd been naughty. She was the one who worried when I got home late, or bollocked me for not doing the washing up. I felt suddenly gutted that I hadn't realised what I'd be sacrificing by moving in with Wyn. That the time had passed when I could chat to her freely.

'I'm fine,' I said, instead.

CHAPTER 21

Everything else faded into the background. College. Sophia and Spencer's taunting. Working at the café. Weekly phone calls with Da (Mam pretending not to be listening in the background). Half-watching a documentary with Wyn, one eye on my phone in case he texted. These were all just intervals. Time with Darsh was the main event.

I'd go to his whenever time allowed. Sometimes we'd be able to sneak away during my lunch break. Other times we'd have to wait until after college. I'd always have to drag myself away from him early evening so I could get home before Wyn started to worry. I'd tell her I'd been at a study group with friends. I stopped going for dunch with Alice after Sunny Side. I told her I had college work to catch up on and spent a few blissful hours with Darsh instead.

When I wasn't with him, I thought about him constantly. How the dips and mounds of the muscles in his arms felt when I ran my hands over the sleeves of his jumper. The way he smelt – a scent I'd never encountered before and found hard to describe, but which was like catnip to me. The triumph I felt when I was able to make him laugh.

Darsh would look at me sometimes like he could see into my soul. It was nothing like how Rhys used to look at me.

I realised, now, that Rhys never properly saw me. He liked it when I wore a full face of make-up, when I'd clipped in hair extensions, applied fake tan and put on short skirts. He used to wear me on his arm as I would wear a handbag – a beautiful thing to show off. Something that reflected his taste.

I still wanted to look pretty for Darsh, but he had different ideas about what beauty was. He liked it when I left my hair unstraightened and let it fall in uneven waves. He sometimes lent me his sweatshirts and, even though they drowned me, he said I looked sexy in them.

He also told me he liked the naturally pale bits on the parts of my body I forgot to fake tan, or couldn't reach. Darsh said it was strange to him that the same white people who treated him like an outsider for having brown skin often artificially darkened their own. He told me that, where he was from, women often lightened their skin. To be paler meant having status, a hangover in attitude after years of being invaded and colonised by the British.

I'd never thought about it like that before. It made me wonder whether there was something disrespectful about fake tan and I stopped applying it.

When I looked in the mirror, a totally new person was beginning to emerge. I liked her. I enjoyed the idea that when I next saw my old friends in Wales, they'd see my transformation.

Darsh asked me questions and, when I answered, actually

listened. Responded as though I was saying something worth listening to.

That was something else I'd been missing, back home. In Wales, I felt like I was always shouting to be understood and constantly being told that what I was thinking was ridiculous. Or a phase. Or just not normal.

Darsh got me. He knew what it was to feel like you were out of sync with everyone around you. He told me he'd felt much the same, back in his hometown. Thoughts I assumed only I'd ever had – like wondering if there'd been a glitch in the Matrix and I'd been living in the wrong family, in the wrong place and time – he said he'd had them too.

One rainy Thursday afternoon, we were lying on his sofa and it occurred to me that, whilst I'd talked about Rhys, we never discussed his exes. I was curious. 'You must have had girlfriends before you met me though?' I asked, squinting up at him from where my head was nestled in his lap.

It was like a shutter came down and instantly he became the cold, closed-off version of himself I'd met the day I spilt coffee over him. He moved my head from his lap and shifted away from me, not meeting my eye.

'Not really,' he said.

I tried to laugh it off, borrowing a line Monica uses in *Friends*. 'How is that possible? Have you seen you?'

He didn't chuckle along with me. Instead, he stood up and said, 'It's getting late. You should go.'

'Don't be like that!' I pleaded.

'I'm not being like anything, Cerys.' He stood so he was

towering above me, stern. I stood too and tried to reach for him, to cup his chin in my hands, but he turned away.

'Fine.' I stomped around his flat noisily picking up my things. I desperately wanted to make it right, to recapture the moment before I'd asked the question, when we'd been cwtching contentedly. But I couldn't work out how to do it. Instead, I just picked up my jacket and left the flat, slamming the door behind me as I went.

Back at Wyn's, I picked at the dinner she'd made – some sort of aubergine thing – and replayed the conversation over and over in my mind. What had I done wrong?

I escaped to bed early, claiming I had a headache, and texted him.

I'm sorry x

Then, when he hadn't replied twenty minutes later, I texted again.

I love you x

We'd never said those words to each other in person, but it had been on the tip of my tongue almost constantly. Something about typing it in a text, combined with the desperation I felt to get his attention and make things between us OK again, gave me the courage to finally admit it.

I stared unblinkingly at my phone for what felt like ages, wondering if he'd read it, imagining all the different reactions he might have, willing him to text back. I must have fallen asleep because the next thing I remembered was pale winter sunlight coming through a gap in the curtains I'd drawn messily the night before and hitting me in the face, startling me awake. The first thing I did was reach for my phone, which was on the pillow next to me. He had replied.

I love you too.

I was so happy I forgot to breathe and had to stick my head out of the window because I felt dizzy.

After the world stopped spinning, I texted him again to arrange to meet after college. In the doorway of his flat, he gathered me into his arms and held me so tightly I squeaked.

'I'm sorry,' he mumbled into my hair.

'No, I'm sorry,' I replied. I wasn't sure why I was saying it, to be honest. I'd only asked a question. I guess I was sorry because it had led to twelve hours of what felt like agony, at least for me.

'Why should you be sorry, Cerys? All you did was ask a question.' Not for the first time, it felt like he was inside my head, seeing my thoughts. As we walked into his now familiar sitting room, he turned to face me. 'It's just hard for me to talk about my past. Painful. You know?'

I didn't really, but his eyes searched mine, anxiously seeking reassurance, and I wanted to give him what he needed. 'I do. Let's just focus on the here and now.'

'The here and now,' he repeated, drawing me to him again and kissing me. I wouldn't have believed it was possible before that point, but our kiss was more intense, more passionate, than any before.

We stumbled backwards and I gasped as my back hit the door we'd just come through. His lips were on my neck now, his hand on my thigh. He pulled my leg up so that it hooked around his waist. I'd never been so turned on in my entire life. I physically ached with horniness. I thought I was going to explode and then melt into a puddle.

Just as I was thinking *this is it, we're going to do it,* he pulled away. He put his hands over his face and breathed like he'd just run a marathon.

'What's wrong?' I asked, realising I was also panting.

'I just . . .' He made an exasperated sound. 'It feels wrong to ask you this after what happened yesterday but . . . Cerys. I need to know. Have you ever had sex before?'

I didn't know what the correct answer was. I knew the truth: I lost my virginity on my sixteenth birthday, to Rhys. We'd done it pretty much every time we'd seen each other between then and when I left for London. But something stopped me from telling Darsh that. I didn't want him to think I was slutty, or to make what was happening between us seem less special. So I lied.

'No.'

Then I added a truth, saying, 'But I want to. With you.'

'I want to as well. You have no idea how much, Cerys. But I think we should wait.'

'Oh. How long?'

'When are you seventeen?'

'In March.' That was months away. I'd explode before then, I was sure of it.

I'd been wanting to ask him exactly how old he was and thought about doing it at that moment but fear of causing another rift between us stopped me. I stared at him, trying to work it out. He couldn't have been more than twenty-one. It wasn't that much of an age gap. Especially since I felt like I was more like eighteen than sixteen. So really, you could argue it was only three years between us. Which was nothing.

I sensed he might be thinking the same thing, but then he said, 'I think we should wait until your birthday.'

My heart sank.

CHAPTER 22

On Sunday, Da rang as usual.

'Your mother has been worrying about the turkey since August,' he said. 'When do you think you'll be back, love?'

I gulped. I really wanted to see him. I missed our Sunday routine of going for a long walk with Gruff through the valleys. Not talking – not needing to. Then coming home and listening to Classic FM while dipping chunks of Dairy Milk into mugs of tea, Da's foot tapping along to the beat of the music. Those days were the only thing I wished I could bring with me from Wales.

Hearing Da's voice made me realise how much I missed him. Yet, there was also so much else to consider. Mam, for a start, who'd hover around us like a dark presence, disapproving. Spoiling everything. And Darsh. I didn't think I could bear to be away from him. Not even for a week.

'Uhm. Well, actually, I was thinking I'll probably stay here for Christmas,' I replied, cringing inwardly as I anticipated his disappointment.

'Really?' He seemed genuinely taken aback, like I'd told him I was going to join the circus, or get a giant tattoo on my face or something.

'Yeah, sorry Da, but I've got lots of college work to do and then there's my job at Sunny Side . . . Plus, Wyn and me are getting along really well,' I gabbled. I knew I wasn't really making any sense. I just needed him to know it wasn't anything to do with him.

'OK then, love. Whatever you think is best. We will miss you though,' he replied sadly. I felt really terrible then. Worse than if he had objected. I briefly considered telling him I'd only been joking. Then I heard Mam being bossy in the background and the impulse deserted me.

'Give me the phone, Dafydd!' I heard Mam demand. There was much rustling and I held Wyn's landline away from my ear in anticipation. It was the right move.

'CERYS BETHAN WILLIAMS! WHAT ON EARTH DO YOU MEAN YOU WON'T BE COMING HOME FOR CHRISTMAS?' she bellowed.

It was the first thing she'd said directly to me since I moved to London and I bristled a bit, wondering why she couldn't resist having a go. She never seemed to have anything kind or positive to say.

'I've made up my mind,' I told her, squashing the slight tremble in my voice. 'You can't bully me into coming back.'

'Bully you? What are you talking about? As if I ever would.' I couldn't see her, but I knew exactly what she'd be doing, in that moment. Her eyebrows would be right up to her hairline and she'd be shrugging at Da as if to say 'what have we done to deserve such a daughter.' It was what she always did when she wanted Da to take her side.

I heard Da saying something in a soothing tone.

'No, I won't! I won't think of it from her point of view, Dafydd! Why can't she think of it from our point of view for once?' She huffed and I heard her pass the phone back to Da.

'She'll come round, leave it with me,' he said. 'Take care of yourself. Bye, love.'

And that was that.

Wyn was out, probably at work. She told me she was planning to spend a few days over Christmas with friends who lived up in Highgate. Since Nain had died, she no longer felt obligated to come back to Wales every year.

'You'd love Tom and his husband, darling,' she told me. 'They always have the most extravagant Christmas tree you've ever seen. And we all play parlour games whilst drinking champagne and eating Marks and Spencer's finger food for three days. It's fabulous.'

It did sound quite fabulous, but I had no interest in the festivities at Tom's. I was going to spend Christmas with Darsh.

I'd have to play it just right, of course. Somehow put Wyn off from checking in with Mam and vice versa. It would be a total pain in the arse, but worth it for Darsh and I to have three whole days of uninterrupted bliss.

Later that day, I told him my plan.

'It will be a yamapuri of our own making,' he said, after I'd explained.

'What do you mean?'

'It means hell.'

'Oh.' This wasn't the reaction I'd expected.

'Or, more accurately, it's purgatory.'

'Is it so terrible, the thought of being with me for more than a couple of hours?' I was starting to get really alarmed, thinking maybe I'd misunderstood. Got something horribly wrong.

'No. That's not what I meant. But Cerys, think about it. You'll be sleeping in my bed. You'll be near me all the time. It is hard enough as it is not to . . . ravish you.'

'Ravish me?' It was such an odd, old-fashioned word for him to have used in that moment. Plus, the way he said it, with a slight roll of the 'r', made it sound extra weird. I burst out laughing.

Darsh looked at me, seeming slightly shocked by my reaction. Something about his serious expression made the whole thing even funnier. Soon, I was shaking with laughter. Then his shoulders relaxed, he started to giggle and we were both in fits.

'I'm sorry,' he said eventually, wiping his eyes. 'I have no idea where that came from. Maybe one of my mum's bad romance novels or something. I used to steal them and read them in bed when I was a kid. Searching for the naughty bits.'

He pulled me to him, so my face was against his chest and his chin was resting on top of my head. I felt him take a very deep breath.

'You know what? Not being near you would be worse,' he said.

'That's what I thought,' I mumbled into his fine-knit sweater.

'I can control myself. It won't be easy, but I can do it.'

As I pressed myself into the contours of his torso, I found myself again wishing that he wouldn't.

***

Darsh didn't celebrate Christmas, which meant I was spared the torture of thinking of a present for him. As Veronica Bailey often wrote in her columns, men were a nightmare to buy for. I used to get Rhys aftershave. I always got Da socks, every year for as long as I could remember. They'd both pretended to be delighted, but we all secretly knew these were boring things to receive. Still, I put the traditional socks for Da and a box of chocolates for Mam in the post a week before Christmas. I got Wyn a fancy Zippo to light her beloved fags with.

I left Wyn's the day before Christmas Eve. Wyn's presents for Mam and Da were in my backpack. I'd think of what to do with them later.

Mam was still annoyed that I wasn't coming back for Christmas, so wasn't speaking to me. I was pretty sure she'd never call Wyn on her mobile and didn't have the number for Tom and his husband's house. My deceit was complete. I could relax, for now.

That wasn't to say they wouldn't talk afterwards and realise I wasn't where they each thought I was over Christmas, but by then I would have had my three days with Darsh. They couldn't exactly turn back time and take those days back. That was all that mattered. I'd deal with any consequences if they came up. Whatever they were, they'd be worth it.

As I took the train to Darsh's, it felt like I was floating. I couldn't stop smiling. I knew the other passengers thought I was being strange, but I didn't care. I grinned until my cheeks hurt and, even then, I couldn't seem to make myself stop.

When I arrived, Darsh showed me the drawer he'd cleared for me to put my things. I thought about that episode of *Sex and the City*, where Carrie can't persuade Big to let her keep some toiletries at his place. She says something about a man's flat being symbolic – if he won't let you have space where he lives it means you're not occupying space in his heart. The drawer must mean Darsh was really committed to me. I placed my belongings in there carefully, thinking he might change his mind if I made a mess.

'Do you want to go to the Christmas market?' Darsh asked.

'You don't do Christmas,' I replied, panicking in case he decided this year he was going to and I hadn't got him a gift.

'No, but you do,' he said. 'And it's interesting to me, as an outsider, to observe British customs and traditions.'

'What if someone sees us?'

'I was thinking we could go to the Southbank. It'll be crowded, full of tourists. No one will know us there.'

I thought about it. Imagined holding Darsh's hand in public, him putting his arm around me, as though we were just like any other couple. The temptation was too strong to resist.

'So, do you want to go?'

'Yes.'

CHAPTER 23

The market on the Southbank was a totally magical experience. Like being inside an actual Christmas card.

There were little wooden huts along the river's edge, selling everything from mince pies to hand-crafted tree ornaments. Each hut had fairy lights strung across it. It was freezing cold and there were people walking around in scarves and bobble hats, clutching paper cups of hot chocolate or mulled wine. It was the Christmassiest thing you could ever think of.

Just like Darsh had said we would be, we were totally anonymous here. Nobody even gave us a second glance.

He had a theory that people who lived in London went back to wherever they came from originally to spend time with their families at Christmas, while everyone else came into London to do stuff like this. He'd seen it happen the previous year, he said. As a newcomer to the city, he liked to watch people and noticed these sorts of things.

People certainly weren't behaving in the way I'd come to associate with Londoners. They were smiling, ambling along as though they had all the time in the world, stopping to point at whatever caught their interest. No one tutted when we got in their way. If London's usual rhythm was The Prodigy, we'd slowed right down to Jamiroquai.

'What do you do for Christmas in Wales?' asked Darsh, as we strolled along clutching each other's gloved hands.

I thought about Christmases past in the old farmhouse back in Llangunnor. I saw it like a painting in my mind. I was sitting on the rug under the low oak beams in the big room downstairs. I was in front of the real log fire, eating a Chocolate Orange. There was a tree in the corner, which Da and I had decorated with paperchains.

Wyn was in an armchair, glass of wine in her hand, ranting about something. Da was sat on the sofa, cracking Brazil nuts into a bowl on his lap, Gruff asleep at his feet. Nain was at the opposite end, asleep in front of a re-run of *Only Fools and Horses.* She loved that show and always called it 'Silly Cockneys'.

Mam was a blurry shape, in my memory. Even at Christmas, she never sat still. Da was always saying to her, 'come and sit down, love,' and she'd reply, 'I will now in a minute. I just have to . . .' And then she'd name a chore: ' . . . finish peeling the potatoes for tomorrow', ' . . . take the rubbish out', ' . . . put a wash on'. It was like she was physically incapable of chilling.

I was suddenly overwhelmed by a totally alien feeling. It was an ache I'd never felt before, somewhere deep in my chest. It took me a while to work out what it was. Homesickness.

But we'd never have another Christmas like the one I'd been remembering, ever again. Nain had been gone for three years. Wyn would rather spend time playing parlour games with

Tom in Highgate. Mam was in a mood with me. Even if I had gone back this year, it would never be the same. I was longing for the ghost of something I'd lost for ever.

I realised Darsh was waiting for me to speak.

'It's just what everyone does, I think,' I said. 'Mam cooks a turkey with all the trimmings. We watch lots of telly. Mam and Wyn usually have an argument about something after one too many sherries.'

Darsh laughed. 'What do they argue about?'

'Everything, if I'm honest. They're so different. Sometimes it's hard to believe they're sisters. Mam's very traditional and Wyn is a massive feminist.'

'And you're more like your aunt?'

'I think so, yeah. I mean . . . I'm not quite as radical as she is. She doesn't seem to like men very much. Apart from the gay ones. And Da. They get on fine.'

'Do you think she would be happier if she was in a relationship?'

I thought about it. I tried to imagine Wyn married, but I just couldn't fathom the type of person she'd want to be with, day in, day out. I didn't think he existed, truth be told.

'No, I don't think so. She likes to live a certain way. Likes her freedom. I can't imagine her compromising on stuff.'

'She must find it difficult having you living with her then?'

The thought had crossed my mind before, but hearing someone else say it was like being slapped in the face.

'She hasn't said so.' I looked at the ground.

'Hey.' He put his finger under my chin, the way he always

did when I was upset or embarrassed. 'I'm sorry, I didn't mean to make you think she doesn't want you there. I just meant . . . well, that it would be better if you tried to stay out of trouble from now on.'

'What do you mean?'

'I mean try to avoid any more incidents like that dreadful photo.'

'I didn't ask to have my photo taken and projected on the wall, you know.'

'I'm not suggesting that you did. I'm just saying it's better not to be vulnerable, if you can help it. Stay with the people you know you can trust.'

'Like you?'

He put his arm around me and pulled me into him. 'Like me.'

We passed a hut selling silver jewellery with vibrant stones. There were bracelets, earrings, rings and pendants, all glistening under the fairy lights. I was mesmerised.

'Pick something,' he said.

'It's OK,' I replied. 'You don't have to.'

'I want to.'

I looked back at the stall. There were pieces with stones of amber, green, turquoise and what looked like a kind of milky diamond.

I touched a ring with one of those pearlescent stones.

'Moonstone,' said the woman in the hut, nodding approvingly. 'Do you want to try it on?'

I did. It was a perfect fit. I moved my hand, watching as flashes of blue sparkled across its pale surface.

'Where I am from,' said Darsh, 'this is the stone that signifies love.'

'Should I choose this one?'

'I think you should. It is perfect.'

I wanted to stay in that moment for ever.

CHAPTER 24

January passed the same way December had – a series of stolen moments with Darsh, and everything in between just a blur. When I wasn't with him I was on autopilot. I was just getting by, doing whatever I had to do to make the time pass so I could be with him again.

I carried on lying to Wyn when I had to, inventing friends I studied with. I told her they lived just around the corner from college whenever she asked why she never saw them.

I made sure I handed in my assignments on time, kept my head down at college, attracted as little attention as possible. Alice asked me to come out with her friends a few more times, but I fobbed her off. She might have even thought I was annoyed with her. But nothing mattered as much as maintaining the delicate balance which meant I could be with Darsh as much as possible.

Before I knew it, it was almost Valentine's Day.

I couldn't avoid getting Darsh a gift – he was my beloved after all – but it was so difficult to know what. He wasn't a particularly sentimental person; there were no framed photos at his flat, no nick-nacks or keepsakes. He didn't have the sort of sense of humour that would appreciate a cheeky novelty gift either. I couldn't afford to get him a cashmere jumper or fancy jeans, which were the only things he ever seemed to wear. I couldn't get him aftershave because I loved the way he smelt so much and didn't want it to change even one tiny bit. Plus, it seemed like a bad omen because it had been my usual gift for Rhys.

I sat there thinking about it for ages and suddenly it hit me. On Diwali, Darsh had cooked for me. He obviously thought that was a nice thing to do for someone. So, I should make him a Valentine's dinner.

There were only two obstacles to my brilliant plan. One was that I couldn't really cook. But how hard could it be? It was just following a recipe and any idiot could do that. The second and more pressing concern was that I'd have to find a way to get Wyn out of the house.

I tried to be subtle at first.

One evening, we were sitting quietly reading (her – a manuscript she was working on, me – *Adept* magazine) and I said, 'You know, you don't have to sit in with me every evening. I don't need babysitting. I feel bad – you must have friends you want to see?'

'Not really, darling,' she replied airily. 'I mean, obviously, one has friends. But we tend to see each other in the summer. We live all over London and it's far too cold to be bothered leaving the house this time of year. And in the meantime, there is the phone.'

Clearly, I needed another plan. The next day, I was on my

way to the library with a very important question I needed to ask Jeeves and I passed the cinema. Inspiration struck.

I scoured the cinema listings for any film showing on the fourteenth of February which looked like it might be up Wyn's street. There was a poster for *Hannibal*, starring Anthony Hopkins. I remember Wyn saying how brilliant he was in the *Mask of Zorro* a couple of years back. Plus, he was Welsh, which meant that Wyn was bound to automatically love him. There was a 7 p.m. showing and I calculated that when you took into account adverts and walking time, I'd probably have about two-and-a-bit hours to make and serve dinner to Darsh. Perfect.

I experienced the familiar frizzle of excitement I still got, even though I'd been told so many times I looked older than I was, when the guy behind the till didn't even hesitate in giving me a ticket for a film with an 18 certificate. That was one problem solved.

I continued on to the library. Once I was settled in front of a computer, I looked around to check no one was lingering close enough to see what was on my screen. Having assured myself they weren't, I nervously typed *Can men tell if you're a virgin?*

The first site that came up was advice on birth control. Not something I needed. I'd had really painful periods and been prescribed the pill to help regulate my hormones when I was fourteen. That reminded me, actually, had I taken my pill that morning? I couldn't remember, with everything going on. I'd check when I got back.

The next was an article about 'virginity tests'.

A virginity test is a practice, usually done by doctors, used to determine whether a woman is still a virgin. The test involves checking whether the woman's hymen is intact. The hymen consists of thin skin which covers the entrance to the vagina . . .

So that would explain why our sex ed teacher had said women bleed the first time they have sex . . . But then, I didn't with Rhys. At the time, I didn't really think about it. I think I was more focused on feeling sort of achy down there and wondering if that meant something was wrong. Rhys told me it was normal and asked me to let him know as soon as I felt better so we could do it again.

I read on . . .

Although it is a procedure dating back to ancient times, it is now widely acknowledged that a hymen can tear for a variety of reasons, including use of tampons and vigorous exercise.

Ah OK. I'd been using tampons for a few years now so that made sense. And if Darsh commented on the lack of blood after we (finally) got down to it then that's what I'd say. I hated that I was having to think of ways to continue the lie I'd told him, but I also knew there was no way to undo it. Not after we'd waited for months and there had been all this build up.

I also just kind of sensed that it meant something to Darsh to be the one I gave my virginity to. I really wished he had been. I had thought I loved Rhys at the time, but when I looked back on it now, it seemed like a stupid sort of fake infatuation. There was no comparison with how I felt about

Darsh. Like Leo says when he first clocks Claire Danes in *Romeo + Juliet*: 'Did my heart love 'til now? Forswear it sight, for I never saw true beauty 'til this night.'

I totally got what he meant.

CHAPTER 25

ADEPT'S GUIDE TO CREATING THE PERFECT VALENTINE'S DAY

The most romantic day of the year is approaching and gone are the times where a simple card was enough to make your beau feel special. Word from the wise is that dining a deux in a restaurant is also old hat. All the chicest couples are staying in.

But you don't want it to descend into a boring evening in front of the telly. (Perish the thought!) You want him to see you as an irresistible sex goddess from the Planet Stunning (obvs). Below is our relationship expert Jenny T's guide to creating a night in you'll both remember . . .

Lighting

Candlelight not only signals romance, but it conceals all your bodily flaws when naked: Bonus!

Heart-shaped candles by Exquisitee: £50 for a pair.

Clothing

Babydolls are so hot right now. Pair them with heels for the ultimate sex kitten look.

'Je t'aime' luxury teddy by NightShade: £142.

Black patent stilettos with five-inch heel by Flavee: £275

Make-up

Less is more. Apply a little concealer, mascara to make your lashes extra fluttery, some blush to give you a sexy flush and of course lip gloss for extra kissable lips.

Stars Concealer in pale beige: £28

Eleganze lengthening mascara in midnight black: £16, LaBelle

'The Big O' natural blush: £27

Stars 'Extra Juicy' lipgloss in pale pink: £17.

Cook

You can't go wrong with steak. All men love it. Fact.

Steak it was then. I borrowed a cookbook from the library with instructions. It looked easy enough – get the pan really hot then fry for a couple of minutes on each side. I'd bung in some oven chips and (hopefully) appear to Darsh as some sort of sophisticated domestic goddess.

I went to the butchers on the Broadway after college and brought two thick, juicy-looking cuts of beef. They cost nearly as much as my wages for the week but it would be worth it. Then I offered to make cups of tea for Wyn all evening so she wouldn't go in the fridge for milk and see the steaks there.

I'd told Wyn the cinema ticket was a thank you for letting me stay and she'd seemed genuinely touched. Of course, I immediately felt guilty about her reaction, because actually I should have bought them for that reason. But she'd never have to know and I seemed to have made her happy. She strutted out of the house, cape flapping behind her, at 6.45. I had fifteen minutes to get myself ready, light the forty tea lights I'd bought in the market for £2 (sorry, Jenny T), fluff the cushions and get the steaks out and brush them with oil and herbs, ahead of Darsh's arrival.

He turned up looking nervous but gorgeous, clutching a small white cardboard box. I'd never seen him look vulnerable before and it made my heart twitch in my chest. I wanted to fling myself on him and cover him in kisses the minute I opened the outer front door. But, even out here in Ealing, there was a chance we could be seen, so I hung back in the hallway and gestured for him to come in.

There was something surreal about seeing Darsh standing

in Wyn's doorway. Two previously separate parts of my life had collided. He placed the box carefully at his feet and shrugged off his heavy coat and boots, putting them neatly by the front door. Rhys would never have thought to do that.

He picked up the box again and handed it to me. 'For you.'

Inside was one big flower. I'd never seen anything like it before. It was squat and kind of flat with green leaves at the base and creamy white petals with pink tips. It looked as though it should be floating on water.

'It's a lotus,' Darsh said, watching me in his intense way. 'Are you pleased?'

'I love it,' I replied, gently cupping the box in both hands, even though I could easily have balanced it on one. Something told me to treat the flower with reverence. I placed it gently on the hall table and took his hand.

'Let me give you a tour,' I said, for some reason. It was a completely ridiculous thing to suggest. Wyn's flat was tiny. Plus, it was the sort of thing Mam would say. I gestured to the left. 'The bathroom is here.' I led him down the corridor and I gestured into the open doorway. 'The kitchen is here.'

I tried to lead him further down the corridor to the sitting room, but felt resistance when I tugged at his hand.

'Cerys,' he whispered, nodding his head in the direction of the kitchen counter, where the two steaks were resting on a chopping board ready to be fried. 'Is that beef?'

'Errr . . . yeah!' I replied, confused by his reaction. He looked really freaked out. There was a moment of silence. I started to gabble in a futile attempt to cover the awkwardness.

'I read . . . somewhere . . . that all men love steak so I went to the fancy butcher on Broadway and he said these are the best and also they're quite easy to cook because I'm not that experienced in the kitchen I mean I can cook obviously but not on this level and I thought it would be romantic and . . .' I paused for breath. 'Do you not like beef?'

'I've never tried it,' he said, still staring at the steaks like they were going to leap off the chopping board and attack him, or something. 'Cows are sacred where I come from. We . . . don't eat them.'

My hands flew to my mouth. 'Oh, god, Darsh – I'm so sorry. I didn't know.'

'Why would you?' He finally looked in my direction, but didn't look me in the eye.

'It's not a big deal! We can order pizza!' My voice sounded slightly hysterical as I swivelled around trying to remember where Wyn kept her pile of takeaway menus.

'It is. It is a big deal, Cerys. This proves that we are from totally different worlds.'

He looked sad now, and I very much did not like the turn this conversation was taking. I felt like he was getting ready to leave and that I had to do whatever possible to not make that happen. I closed the kitchen door. It had remained permanently open for as long as I could remember and emitted a squeaking noise, as though startled to be called into service after so many years.

Then I stepped towards Darsh and reached for his face.

'We're both outsiders in London,' I reminded him, thinking

back to all the conversations we'd had about how out of place we both felt here. How those chats had bonded us. 'I can learn the other stuff.'

I could see he had gone somewhere else in his head. He was slipping away from me and I needed him to come back. So, I stood on my tiptoes and kissed him softly, stroking the hair at the nape of his neck because I knew he liked that.

I felt his body respond. As though by instinct, his hands were around my waist, holding me as tightly as he always did – like I might disappear if he didn't. Our kiss deepened, becoming frantic, and I got that now-familiar floaty feeling, as though I was dissolving into him somehow.

I had his attention now, but somewhere in the back of my mind an alarm bell was ringing. We'd kissed like this hundreds of times before. It might not be enough to silence his doubts and to keep him here. So, I grabbed the hem of his sweater and started to lift it over his head.

'Cerys!' he gasped. 'What are you doing?'

'It's OK,' I replied, as I succeeded in removing his jumper and T-shirt in a fairly seamless move. I congratulated myself for making the gesture sexy at the same time as reminding myself not to appear too experienced. I took in his broad shoulders and his gorgeous brown skin, which was glowing in the candle light. I resisted the urge to run my hands over his chest, sensing that I needed to go slowly if my plan was going to work.

Darsh was watching me, his dark eyes gleaming. I slipped the straps of my dress off my shoulders and let it fall to the ground in a silky puddle around my feet. I'd worn nice underwear, just in case.

I saw something in Darsh's eyes change as he grabbed me again. The feeling of his skin against mine was exquisite. I threw my head back, feeling the ends of my hair tickle the skin below my bra strap as Darsh kissed my neck. This was it. He was locked in now. I'd made him stay. He was mine.

I noticed the sound of keys in the lock before he did. I tried to push him off, to think of some way I could hide him, but there wasn't enough time. Wyn was chattering loudly as she stepped into the hallway, already halfway through removing her cape.

'I'm sorry, darling, forgot my glasses. Couldn't see a th—'

She stopped mid-sentence and gasped.

None of us spoke. There was nothing we could say. There was no way Darsh or I could explain away the sight that greeted Wyn. There simply was no innocent excuse.

I hardly dared breathe, let alone reach for my dress to cover myself. I just stood, statue-like, feeling nervous goose pimples erupting across the surface of my skin.

It was Wyn who finally broke the silence. Her voice was eerily calm. She was looking only at Darsh.

'Kindly dress yourself and get out.'

CHAPTER 26

After Darsh had bolted out of the door, knocking the box containing the lotus flower off the table in his haste, Wyn talked at me for what felt like a year. The weirdest thing, though, was that she didn't seem angry. At least not with me.

'Now, don't worry, darling,' she'd said as she wrapped her arms around my shoulders and led me into the sitting room. 'I will help you deal with this.'

I sat in one of the armchairs, not trusting myself to speak. I watched as she paced up and down in front of me, ranting about men and patriarchy and how she thought we'd left all this kind of thing behind in the 1970s.

'I am going to make sure that justice is done here. But I'm going to need you to be honest with me. I need to know . . . Has he had sex with you?'

'No!' I exclaimed, feeling indignant even though that was exactly what I had wanted to happen.

'But he has . . . touched you?'

There was no point in denying that. She'd seen it. I nodded.

'First thing tomorrow, I'm going to telephone that principal. I don't know whether this is a criminal or a civil matter, given that you are above the age of consent. Perhaps he can advise—'

'Wyn!' I interrupted her before I'd thought what my next words were going to be, horrified at the prospect of her getting Darsh into trouble at the college. About five thousand things I could say whirred around my mind like a fruit machine before it settled on *just tell the truth*. Or a version of it, anyway.

'It isn't what you think. Darsh is my boyfriend. I love him.'

'Oh, darling.' Wyn perched herself on the arm of the chair and took my hand in hers. 'I didn't realise things were this bad. You might think you love him, but love doesn't involve an abuse of power. He is your teacher.'

'No, he isn't! He just does guest lectures at the college sometimes. I've never even been in one of his classes. And he's only young. I'm nearly seventeen . . .'

'He looks as though he is in his early twenties. That's a huge gap at your age. It's hard to explain, darling, but people in their twenties think very differently from the way you do now.'

'Oh my god! Stop patronising me!' I stood up, my sudden movement startling Mooch. He leapt out of the other armchair, which he had been curled up in, snoozing as usual.

'I always thought you were so cool,' I continued, knowing I was hitting Wyn where it would hurt her but, being so angry, I didn't particularly care. 'But you're not even listening to me. You're acting like an old fuddy-duddy. Like Mam!'

Wyn took a deep breath in through her nose. It was excruciating, waiting for whatever she was going to say next.

'OK, darling, explain it to me from your point of view.'

So I did. I told her that when I'd first met Darsh we weren't even on college grounds. How he'd been so supportive of me when that terrible thing happened with the photograph. I skipped the part where I stayed at his flat after the night where my drink was spiked, sensing this might cause her to freak out again, just when she seemed to be really listening.

I made sure to emphasise how I was the one who had pushed for our friendship to turn into something more. I'd fancied him from the moment I saw him. I'd been the one to kiss him first.

'It still doesn't sit right with me, darling,' Wyn said, lighting a fag and looking up at the ceiling as she exhaled smoke in its direction.

'OK, look at it this way,' I said. 'Do you really think if you tell the principal, he's going to see it the same way you do? Think about what he was like in that meeting, back before Christmas. The guy's a massive sexist. He'll blame me. I'll get expelled. I'll have to go back to Wales and this whole thing will be a failure and I don't think I could stand that, Wyn. I love it so much here.'

The last part wasn't strictly true. It was Darsh I loved more than London, but it seemed like Wyn was softening. I was flattering her into submission.

'I can't let you continue living here and seeing that man.' Wyn seemed genuinely sad to have to tell me this. 'It wouldn't be right.'

'OK, so, what if I promised not to see him again?' Wyn

looked dubious. 'Seriously! Like I said, it's not like he is my teacher. He's barely at the college. He'd be easy enough to avoid.'

I had absolutely no intention of giving up Darsh, but there was no reason Wyn should have to know that. We'd just have to be careful. Even more cautious than before.

'Didn't you say you loved him?'

Balls. I forgot I'd told her that. 'I . . . thought I did.'

Wyn raised one eyebrow. This was a weak argument and we both knew it.

'OK, so thinking about it, maybe it was a rebound thing? I've only just broken up with Rhys. Darsh was there and he is hot. Even you said so yourself.'

'Darsh, is it? You know that means "handsome" in Sanskrit?' Wyn could never resist the urge to show off her vast knowledge of words, even in the middle of a crisis.

'Well, there you go. What is that thing you told me about again, where a person's name matches who they are?'

'Nominative determinism, darling.' We both laughed. This was great. I was definitely wearing her down.

'Although it's not strictly their name matching how they are. More the job they do. Anyway, the point is, he is handsome, this Darsh. But he is also dangerous. For you, I mean. I need you to understand that I am serious about this.'

'I do! I totally do. I'm sorry I let you down. It won't happen again.'

'I want you to come straight back here after college. Every day.'

'I will.'

'And if he contacts you again, you are to tell me straight away.'

'OK.'

'And if you change your mind. If you reflect on what's gone on and decide that actually you feel . . . exploited in some way, you know you can tell me?'

'I do.'

'And to be absolutely clear, Cerys, if I ever even hear so much of a whisper of you seeing that man again, I will have to get your parents involved. I mean it this time.'

I gulped. 'Understood.'

'OK.' She stood to face me and gave me a hug. 'I am probably an idiot, but I am choosing to trust you, darling. Don't let me down.'

'I won't,' I replied solemnly. I felt a sick sensation in my lower belly as the guilt of so much lying twisted my guts.

Later, I sat listening to fat droplets of rain hurl themselves against the glass of my bedroom window, thinking about the best way to play this situation. How could I make it better? Finally, I texted Darsh.

Have talked my aunt around. She is cool but we have to be extra careful from now on. Sorry about tonight. Love you.

Then I deleted every single message we had ever exchanged from my phone and changed his name in my contacts to Alice. I lay back on my bed and looked at the ceiling. The dark whisper of a terrible thought pushed at the edges of my mind.

What I had just told Darsh had been a lie. That meant I was now lying to everyone I knew.

I pushed it away. It didn't matter. Nothing mattered, as long as I had him.

CHAPTER 27

Wyn's orders that I should come home straight after college every day forced me to bunk off if I wanted to see Darsh. Whenever he wasn't busy or working we'd spend the day together, usually about twice a week. The days in between felt like torture, as I wondered endlessly what he was doing and whether he was thinking about me too.

I made sure to sign in on the mornings of the Darsh days, so my name would be on the register and Wyn wouldn't receive a phone call telling her I was skiving.

My tutor tapped me on the shoulder as I was leaving one morning.

'Another free period, Cerys?'

'Uhm . . . yeah.' I smiled uncomfortably.

'Just wanted to remind you it's about time to start thinking about your final project.'

We had to create something by the end of the summer term. A piece of art which used techniques we'd been learning throughout the year. I nodded, but barely registered it, my mind so full of thoughts of Darsh that there wasn't much room for anything else. When I was in class, I'd sit there daydreaming about him. As often as I could without my tutors getting suspicious, I'd sneak away to his place, making sure to wear a hat and a hood just in case I was recognised.

We had sex the first time we saw each other again after Valentine's Day. The drama of what happened made everything feel more intense and like we had to seize the moment. There were still a few weeks to go until my seventeenth birthday, but it was like the age gap didn't matter so much to Darsh any more. It had never really mattered to me.

I was trying to second-guess myself the whole way through the sex, thinking about what I would do if I was still a virgin. I was trying to act like I didn't know what would happen if I touched what, or which bit came next. I was having to squash all my instincts, not grab his thing and stroke it as we kissed in case it seemed like I'd done it before. Not reach behind my back and undo my bra from behind because why would you ever have done that unless it was in front of another person? When girls are alone they swivel their bras around before they unhook them, everyone knew that.

I was trying to remember my first time with Rhys. I am sure there were things I just . . . did, whether through instinct or because I'd read so many issues of *Adept* with its tips on how to please your man. But the version of myself I was with Darsh was different – more innocent but also more sophisticated, somehow.

Darsh's Cerys didn't enjoy reading about sex in magazines or date boys her own age or give them hand jobs. All that was beneath her.

I'm sure it was my play-acting that resulted in the sex being . . . if not *bad* exactly, not as incredible as I would have ideally liked. I don't know how to explain it, really, other than to say it was a bit . . . clunky. We did it in Darsh's bed, under the covers, and there was none of the spontaneous passion of the times we'd kissed before. I didn't get the melty feeling like I was crackling with energy. I suppose, after spending so many hours daydreaming and fantasising about the moment, it was never going to live up to my expectations.

Just as we were reaching the bit where he was going to go inside me (which I wasn't supposed to know was happening because I was, after all, a 'virgin') Darsh said, 'It is time for me to get a condom.'

'It's OK,' I said, 'I'm on the pill.' He looked at me, startled.

'I've been on it since I was fourteen. Not for contraception. For . . . other reasons.' Why was this conversation so difficult? We'd talked about our innermost fears, hopes and dreams together, so why couldn't I say 'period' in front of him?

'You're sure?'

I nodded. Pausing to get a condom now would just make everything even more awkward and I wanted Darsh to have a good time. A brief memory of some soap in which a character had talked about how condoms were the only way to protect against STIs flashed across my brain. I dismissed it. Darsh was so clean and wholesome. There was no way he had anything.

When I'd imagined Darsh pushing into me for the first time, we'd always been looking into each other's eyes like they do in romantic films. It wasn't like that in reality.

Instead, he'd buried his face into my neck and entered me with such force it made me yelp.

'I'm sorry,' he mumbled.

'It's OK,' I whispered in reply, embarrassed that I hadn't controlled myself better. 'I'm OK. Please carry on.'

So, he did. And it was . . . fine. He was still the hottest person I'd ever laid eyes on, after all. I loved him and he was making love to me. Mostly I just felt lucky.

I calculated that, if I really was a virgin, we'd probably have to have done it about four or five times before I'd get into the swing of it. So, I waited, even though it was frustrating to have to carry on having really average sex. Then, one day when we were sitting on the sofa, I climbed on to his lap and straddled him. I rubbed my chest against his and kissed him just below his ear. I made an 'mmmm' sound, because Rhys used to like it when I did that. Darsh's hands had been on my thighs, but then, abruptly, he moved them to my waist and lifted me off of him.

'I don't want to do it like this,' he'd said, when I looked at him questioningly.

'What did I do wrong?' I asked, trying to hide how wounded my pride felt by his rejection.

'Just . . . writhing around like you're in a hip-hop video. It's not sexy to me, Cerys. I like it when you are yourself.'

Two thoughts hit me simultaneously. One, that it was such a sweet thing of him to say. The other, that, in that moment, I had no idea who 'myself' was.

Later that evening, I sat with Wyn while she flicked through the *Radio Times*. This was our ritual. She'd read out the listings of what was on TV that evening and we'd debate what we would watch based on various criteria. These included what mood we were each in and how much we'd learn from it. Wyn had also taught me about something called the Bechdel test, which measured how much female characters spoke and what percentage of their time they were spending discussing men when they did.

'Oooh!' she said. 'They're showing *The Silence of the Lambs* later.'

'Isn't that in the same series as . . .' I trailed off, not finishing the sentence by saying 'the film I bought you a ticket to see the night you caught me about to have sex in your hallway'.

'Yes, darling.' Wyn glossed over the awkwardness. 'You would have been too young to watch *The Silence of the Lambs* when it came out. 91 I think it was . . . It's a psychological thriller. Very clever, actually.'

'Oh, yeah?' I said, only half-listening. I was turning Darsh's words about what made me attractive over and over in my mind. Wondering how I could be more of what appealed to him. Trying to create a character in his image. Imagining what she would wear. How she would speak. What she would talk about.

Wyn interrupted my thoughts by breaking into one of her hacking coughs. She'd always had an annoying smoker's cough for as long as I could remember, but recently it seemed to be getting worse. The coughing fits were more frequent, and longer, louder, more violent. I was worried about her.

'Do you think you should go and see a doctor about that?'

'I will, darling.' She waved my concerns away. 'Anyway,

what were we talking about? Oh yes, *The Silence of the Lambs* . . . There's a scene I'll never forget. The serial killer has this woman as his hostage. He keeps her in a hole in the ground, too deep for her to escape. And he calls her "it". Saying "*it* does this" when he wants her to do something. And she keeps telling him details about her life. Like her name. Who her father is, I think. Anyway, the point is she knows he won't be able to kill her if he acknowledges that she is a person.'

'That's quite clever. Of her, I mean. To think of that in such a scary moment,' I remarked.

'Well, the film is also making a wider feminist point, I think. About violence against women. If women weren't objectified all the time, if they were seen as people rather than things, it would be a lot harder for men to hurt them.'

Wyn had my full focus now. The seed of an idea was starting to form in my mind.

'Wyn . . . Sorry to ask, but have you bought me a birthday present yet?'

'Actually, no, not yet, darling. Your parents and I had an idea about clubbing together to get you something you really need. It's not like you have a lot of room here so we thought that would be better than getting you smellies, or jewellery or whatever. But there was some . . . disagreement over what would be the best thing for us to buy. Do you know what you want then?'

'I do. I've just thought of it. And actually, it works really well as a joint present with Mam and Da.'

'Go on then, darling. Out with it.'

'I'd like a camera.'

CHAPTER 28

I'd never had a proper camera before. Whenever we went on holiday, Da used to buy a disposable one from the chemist. He called it a 'point and shoot'. They were flimsy plastic things with a wheel on the back you had to slide with your thumb between each shot. The wheel made a sort of crunchy, squeaky sound which was weirdly quite satisfying. You could buy ones that took twenty-four photos or thirty-six.

With a point and shoot, you literally aimed it at the thing you wanted to take a photo of, pressed the button and kept doing that until the roll of film inside ran out. Then, you took it back to the chemist and one week later they'd give you a little cardboard envelope full of the photos you'd taken. Most of them were blurry and on the wonk, but you'd have maybe five that were really good and those were the ones you stuck in photo albums or bought frames for.

The camera my parents and Wyn bought me for my birthday was completely different. It was about five times the size of a point and shoot, for a start, and much heavier. It had a round lens poking out of it and you could zoom in and out using buttons at the back. Below the buttons was a small window, so you could see what you were photographing. And, best of all, there was a strap so you could wear it around your neck. Like a fashion accessory, but one with a function other than to make you look ten per cent prettier.

I soon got completely addicted to using it. One of the tutors at college got really excited when she saw me with it. I'd not had any classes with her before, but she introduced herself as Kate and talked me through how to use the functions properly. Then, she showed me how to develop my shots in the dark room right at the back of the building. I'd never even noticed it was there before.

Spending time with Kate, developing my photos, was the single funnest thing I'd ever done in my life. We dipped sheets of shiny photographic paper in trays of special fluid then hung them up using pegs, on string which stretched from one side of the room to the other. There was something really soothing and satisfying about the whole process. I even found I wasn't skipping college to be with Darsh as much as I had been.

Darsh didn't seem to mind. In fact, he encouraged me to spend time in the dark room. He smiled and nodded like I'd said something wise when I told him I didn't feel like I had to dress up as much because just having the camera made me feel interesting. It was a relief to be with someone so mature and understanding. Rhys would definitely have been jealous.

I took photos of everything that caught my eye. Two old men chatting and laughing at a rickety pavement table outside a café, in a way that kind of reminded me of Da. Close-ups of flowers that grew on the small squares set back from the pavements around Chelsea and Fulham. Anyone wearing an interesting outfit. Kate said some of my photos were really good, but I knew they were all just practice. I was honing my skills ready to take one specific shot. One I'd been picturing in my mind ever since Wyn and I had talked about *The Silence of the Lambs* back in March.

I must have taken hundreds of photos that spring. When I looked back on my earliest shots I could see I was getting better. Or 'more accomplished', as Kate would say. Then, one day, I just felt ready.

'Remind me what we are doing here again?' asked Alice, as we made our way through Chelsea one warm afternoon in June. It was a Saturday, we'd just finished our shift and were headed to Spencer's house.

'It's for my end of year art project,' I told her, for about the twelfth time. 'But since I'm the subject of the portrait, I need someone else to actually take the photograph.'

'Don't I need to have some kind of . . . special skills to do that?' Alice looked worried. 'You know I'm a scientist, right? My artistic talents are, let us say, limited.'

'You don't need to do anything special,' I assured her. 'I'll set up the shot. You just need to hold the camera still and press the button. If I had a tripod I could put it on timer and do it myself. But I don't, so . . .'

'So, what you're saying is I'm basically a human tripod?' Alice laughed.

'Yeah, sorry. But, like I said, dunch afterwards is on me. Where do you want to go?'

'Anywhere but Sunny Side Up. Honestly, I've been eating so many of my meals there recently to avoid spending beyond my student loan. If I have to eat one more sausage and bacon bap I will actually turn into a pig.'

She snorted and I laughed.

We reached the steps outside Spencer's house. I was pretty sure he wouldn't randomly look out of the window at the exact moment I did what I was planning to do, but I also didn't want to take any chances.

'We'll have to be quite quick when we take the actual photo,' I told her.

'Gotcha. My finger is ready whenever you need it. OK, that sounds wrong.'

I laughed again. I was so glad Alice had agreed to do this. I thought it might be awkward to ask her after turning down her offers to go out, but she'd said yes without hesitating. Now I thought about it, I couldn't imagine her holding a grudge. There was something about Alice that made you think she was truly in the moment. She was a complete contrast to Darsh, who always had creases in his forehead where he was overthinking everything.

Later, we sat tucking into chicken quesadillas at a Mexican place I had often walked past on my way to and from college and wanted to try.

'God, I love sour cream. If sour cream was a person I'd marry her,' Alice said, licking the back of her spoon.

'As long as salsa is still single, because I've got dibs on him,' I replied.

'So, tell me something about you I don't know already,' Alice said, when we paused in devouring our meals to catch our breath.

'What do you want to know?'

'Anything! OK . . . If you were a biscuit, what biscuit would you be?'

I burst out laughing. 'Biscuit?'

'Hey, you can tell a lot about someone by what biscuit they'd be. I reckon I'm a Hobnob, by the way.'

'Oh, yeah? What's led you to that conclusion?'

'I'm not much to look at, but when people get to know me I usually become a reliable favourite.' She grinned.

'Oh, come on. You're really pretty!'

She blushed. 'Come on then, what biscuit are you?' she pressed me. 'And don't say a Party Ring.'

'Why not a Party Ring?'

'All style, no substance. Everyone likes the idea of them but they're always the last left in the selection box, along with the pink wafers. You're better than that.'

'Wow, you've really thought about this. OK . . . I think I'm a . . . custard cream!'

'Interesting. Why is that?'

'I have no idea,' I admitted. 'It just felt right when I thought it in my head, so I said it.'

Alice narrowed her eyes at me and pointed her fork in my direction. 'I think you are definitely a custard cream. There's layers to you.'

Now it was my turn to blush.

'Hey, did I tell you – I'm seeing someone,' Alice suddenly burst out, in a way that made it obvious she'd been dying to say it all afternoon.

'You didn't say. What's she like?' I asked.

'Well, we haven't been a thing for long, so you can absolutely not remind me of this in a month's time when I'll probably be crying over her into a tub of Häagen-Dazs, but so far she is pretty perfect.'

'Who does she look like? Give me a celebrity example.'

'Oh, I don't know. No one you'd think is attractive, probably. Straight women have such odd ideas about what makes other women hot.'

'Like how?' I was intrigued.

'Well, for a start you don't have to be incredibly thin to be beautiful. Don't get me wrong, if that's your body type then it can look great,' Alice added quickly, perhaps realising that she was talking to a naturally slim person. 'But so many women seem to think they have to starve themselves until they look like one of the cast of *Friends*, or something.'

I tried to think of one single woman considered beautiful who wasn't also incredibly skinny and failed.

'And this idea that you have to have enormous perfectly round tits that look like melons is also stupid.' Alice was on a roll now.

'OK, now you're talking my language.' I laughed.

'It's hard to describe why I like Simone – that's her name, by the way. It's the essence of her I'm drawn to. God, I sound like a poncy poet. Sorry.'

'No, I like it! It's nice that you're happy. So, are you official?'

'Yeah, we've had the exclusivity chat.' Alice's eyes were shining. She really had it bad.

'And you've told her that I'm straight? And that you don't fancy me?'

'Why would I do that?'

'I just thought . . . maybe she might not like you being out with another girl.'

'Well, it's not like I'm cheating on her, is it?'

'No.'

'So, what do you mean?' I wished Alice wouldn't badger me to explain like this. I felt really stupid now.

'I'm not sure,' I answered honestly. 'I guess . . . Every guy I've been with wouldn't have been happy if I had male friends.' In fact, Darsh didn't like me having friends of any gender. To keep me safe, he said.

'That's an indication that they're insecure.' Alice gave a knowing nod. 'And you should run a mile. But you know that, right?'

'Uhmmm . . .'

'Well, OK, now you know it. Henceforth, you shall make better choices. It hath been decreed, by me!' Alice waved her spoon around like it was a wand. 'Speaking of which, are you seeing anyone at the moment? The college boys must be wild for you?'

Part of me wanted to tell her the whole thing. Get it all out there, like a confession – how Darsh and I had been secretly seeing each other for seven months now. How our romance was forbidden. How that made me feel like Claire Danes to Darsh's Leo. How it had been so exciting, at first. How hard I'd fallen for him and how fast.

I wanted to share the excitement of our relationship with someone. To listen to Alice say 'ooh!' as I described just how sexy and secret it had all been. I wanted to feel interesting and exotic and daring.

I also wanted to confide in her how, lately, I'd started to feel like something had shifted between Darsh and I. He didn't look at me like he could see into my soul any more. He didn't squeeze me so tightly it knocked all of the breath out of my lungs.

It would have been a relief to tell another human how scared I was of losing him. Alice was a little older than me and much wiser. Maybe she knew what it was like to spend hours wondering what went wrong in a relationship and why. Imagining ways to fix it. Losing yourself in memories of when things were perfect and wishing you had the power to turn back time.

But I also thought she might not know what I was talking about. Girls obviously behaved differently to boys, in relationships. Or worse, maybe she'd think I was young and stupid and start to pity me.

So, I didn't share any of my secrets with Alice. I kept them locked away, where they had been hiding for months, away from the judgment of others.

Instead, I just shrugged and said, 'No, not at the moment.'

***

After Alice and I hugged each other goodbye and promised to meet up again soon, I wasn't in any particular hurry to get back to Wyn's.

It was starting to feel claustrophobic at her place. Every time I picked up my phone to send a text I could feel her watching me. I imagined she was having to stop herself from asking who it was to. Wondering if it was him. The constant noise of her coughing fits was also really starting to grate on me.

I wandered into a newsagent and looked at the shelves of magazines. I'd already inhaled that month's *Adept*, so I turned my attention to the celeb weeklies. I picked one up at random and started leafing through it. There were the usual pictures of It girls and actresses outside clubs.

CLAUDIA'S NIP SLIP!

read one caption.

HAS TARA BEEN
PILING ON THE POUNDS?

read another.

There was a ring around the subject's midriff, highlighting her supposed weight gain.

By the time I got to a caption saying

WORSE FOR WEAR CLAIRE

I realised these pictures were hitting me differently than they used to. I used to enjoy poring over spreads like this, seeing famous people looking less than perfect. It made me feel better about myself.

But now I had been snapped without my consent, I knew how these women felt. They weren't just exposed boobs and slightly-bigger-than-usual stomachs and eyes half closed in apparent drunkenness to me now. They were people with stories and emotions and, perhaps most importantly, a right to privacy.

I felt a wave of nausea sweep over me. I'd thought what happened with the photo at college was a one-off injustice, but it was actually something that happened every day. Something that was probably happening right now. And I'd been part of it. A paying audience member witnessing the circus.

I threw the *Celebrity Clarion* back on the shelf, left the newsagent and went into a chemist in search of one of my other favourite treats: some new make-up.

Mam always said she could not understand my ability to fritter away a whole afternoon looking at cosmetics, but it was one of my favourite things to do. I loved anything with glitter. I also liked fun colours – purple liners which complemented my grey eyes, or deep burgundy lip glosses which stood out against my blonde hair. I used to wear them all the time, but Darsh said he preferred me to look natural.

Sighing, I picked up a muted eyeshadow duo, consisting of a boring beige and barely there brown. That would have to do.

As I walked to the counter to pay, I walked past the aisle with shelves full of tampons and towels. It reminded me that I was meant to be on my period. It was the week between pills.

In fact, it was day five. Why hadn't my period come?

I stopped in my tracks and gasped. I couldn't be, could I?

My vision blurred and I suddenly felt dizzy. Then I caught myself. I was overreacting. It was bound to be fine. People had missed periods for no reason all the time. Now I thought about it, I'd run two packets of pills together without a break when I first started having sex with Darsh so my bodily functions wouldn't interrupt our fun. His fun. That had probably thrown my cycle out of sync.

I'd been really stressed too, running around trying to conceal my tracks by lying to everyone. I read somewhere that stress can stop your period arriving.

Still, though, a voice in my head reasoned, *you should get a test, just to be sure.*

I wandered up and down, trying to look for the family planning section without being too obvious. When I located it, somewhere at the back near those disgusting milkshakes people drink when they're trying to lose weight, it was just about forty different brands of condoms.

I was going to have to ask someone. I saw a woman wearing a tabard emblazoned with the logo of the shop. She was stacking rows and rows of vitamin supplements. All I had to do was tap her on the shoulder and say, 'Excuse me, where are your pregnancy tests?'

But I just didn't think I could say the words out loud. It was too embarrassing. I might as well just march up to her and say, 'Hello! I've been having loads of sex and have been too stupid to take proper precautions!' And what if someone overheard? What if someone from college just happened to be in the next aisle? I'd die of shame.

I ran out of the shop and down the road until a burning in my lungs forced me to stop. It was only when I put my hands on my thighs to catch my breath that I realised I was still holding the hideous eyeshadow duo.

Now I could add shoplifting to my list of reasons to feel guilty.

CHAPTER 29

I sat on the toilet, the white, blood-free cotton of my knickers stretched between my knees, willing my period to come. If it would just arrive, then I could stop holding my breath.

For the first time since I was about five, I prayed.

'Please God, if you exist, help me. I know I've been stupid but I've learnt my lesson. I promise, if you help me, I'll start being more careful. I'll take my pill at the same time every day. I'll make Darsh wear condoms. Whatever you want. Just make this right.'

Then, I filled the washing up bowl with warm, soapy water and cleaned Wyn's windows in case Hinduism had it right and karma existed. I was willing to try anything at this point.

It was like God had heard me and wanted to send me a message. Only, it was the wrong one. The next morning, I woke up with what I can only describe as 'jugs'. I remember some girls at school saying it was like their breasts had suddenly developed overnight when they went through puberty, but in my case it had actually happened.

I was used to not giving my tits much consideration. Bras were a decorative thing, for me. Optional, rather than necessary for support. But that morning, my chest felt heavy and ached. Like a dull period pain, but further up. And my breasts looked to me as though they had doubled in size. When I stood naked in front of the tiny bathroom mirror before taking my morning shower I felt as though I'd suddenly turned into Jordan.

Still, I told myself, it was probably a freak occurrence. Maybe I was going through some kind of weird hormonal blip. A pregnancy test would just be a formality, to calm my mind down.

I couldn't do it alone though. I needed backup. And there was only one person I could think of who I could confide in. Who could hold my hand without creating a giant drama. Alice.

I'd avoided telling Darsh about when Alice and I had hung out the other day. It wasn't a full lie. I just didn't mention I'd seen her. I knew what he'd say – I didn't know her well enough. She might be another Sophia. What if something awful happened to me again?

He was only being protective, but I just didn't believe Alice was like that. Yet, hanging out with her made me feel like I was somehow cheating on Darsh.

This could potentially become a problem if I wanted to carry on being Alice's friend. It was such a mess. Being with Darsh meant lying to Wyn and the college. Being friends with Alice meant lying to Darsh. And Alice didn't even know about Darsh. There was no one I could be completely honest with.

The irrational thought burrowed into my head that maybe

I was being punished for something. How was I supposed to undo it though? I couldn't come clean to everyone without totally detonating my life. I was in too deep.

I tortured myself with these thoughts for almost a week. They looped round and round in my head like clothes in a washing machine until I wanted to knock myself out with a brick just to make them stop.

Finally, Saturday and my shift at Sunny Side arrived. I waited until Alice took her first break and went to find her in the stairwell. I squished myself on the step next to her.

'What's wrong?' she asked, her mouth full of bacon and sausage bap. 'Oh, fuck, is Sally here? Bloody typical, just as I take my break. Hang on, I'll just snarf this and then I'll be with you . . .'

'It's not that.'

'What then? Are you OK? Who's watching the counter?'

'No one. I'll go back in a second. I just have to ask you something.'

'OK . . .' Alice's voice became soft. I wondered if I looked as freaked out as I felt.

I gulped a few times, not sure if I had the courage to say what needed to be said. Wondering if I could get away with just saying 'we've run out of cheese slices' instead. When I was finally able to get the words out, they came out in a strange, fast jumble.

'I need to buy a pregnancy test.'

'Oh.'

'I tried to get one before, but I couldn't do it. My period is late.

My boobs hurt. I just need to know. But I'm scared. Will you come with me?'

'Listen, hun.' She put her arm around my shoulder and gave it a little squeeze. 'You're probably not pregnant. Every straight woman I know has had a scare like this at some point and it turned out to be nothing.'

I nodded, looking at my knees, not quite able to meet her eye.

'But,' she went on, 'just to be sure, we should do a test.' I loved her, in that moment, for saying 'we'. Like it was both of our problem.

'And of course I'll come with you. In fact, if you want, I'll go in and get it for you. I don't mind. Be nice to vicariously experience hetero life.' Her laugh sounded forced and I could tell that she was doing her very best to make me feel better and put me at my ease. She was being so kind and I was grateful for that, so I made myself laugh along with her.

'Thank you.'

I couldn't concentrate for the rest of my shift. I spilt a customer's cappuccino in their lap. I gave another mushroom risotto when they'd clearly asked for egg and chips. I felt like I was in a daze, and simple things, like adding up a ham omelette and a Diet Coke, were too much for me. One guy called me a stupid bimbo when I accidentally short-changed him.

'Oi!' Alice shouted. 'Talk to a member of staff like that again and you'll be barred. FOR LIFE!'

He slunk away, muttering to himself.

'Whatever happened to the "customer's always right"?' I asked Alice, thinking about the fourteen billion times

I'd been told this during my induction training.

'Bollocks,' said Alice. 'More often than not, the customer is an entitled douchenozzle.'

My laugh was genuine this time, despite everything playing on my mind.

When our shift finally finished, Alice strolled into the nearest chemist like it was nothing and emerged a few minutes later brandishing a long, slim box. I grabbed it quickly, stuffing it into my bag. I knew Wyn was out somewhere and, being not too far from home, had horrors of bumping into her while clutching the pregnancy test.

'Thank you so much,' I said. 'I feel like I should do something for you to say thank you. Can I buy you dunch?' I was hoping she would say no because I was desperate to go home and do the test. Get it out of the way. Prove to myself that I really was worrying about nothing.

'Maybe another time,' Alice replied, half-smiling in a sympathetic way. 'For now, why don't you go home and take the test? Put your mind at ease?'

I was so grateful to Alice I could have kissed her, had that not been a wildly inappropriate thing to do.

Less than half an hour later, I was sat on the edge of the bath with my head between my legs, trying desperately to summon a coherent thought.

Two blue lines.

I tried to tell myself it was a faulty test. That must happen sometimes. I'd get another one, somehow. Buy myself more time. But somewhere deep down I knew. I just . . . knew.

What the hell was I going to do?

Wyn had interrupted my spiralling thoughts when she came home. There was no way I could hide what a state I was in. I'd have to tell her. As much as I was dreading the prospect, I also thought it might be a relief.

When I found her in the kitchen, though, she was in an even worse state than I was.

'Darling,' she whispered, her voice quiet and somehow dry-sounding. It was so different to how she usually spoke. 'I'm afraid I've had some bad news. I'm dying.'

I spluttered out a laugh, thinking she must be playing some kind of weird practical joke. Or maybe exaggerating for comic effect because she had a cold or something. She didn't join in, just carried on staring but without seeming to see anything.

'What?' I said finally. 'What do you mean?'

'Exactly what I said. I just came back from the hospital. I have been given six months at most.'

'Is this a joke?'

'No, darling,' she looked at me, not even the whisper of a smile on her face. 'I am afraid not.'

'What's wrong with you?' I should have found a more sensitive way to phrase the question, but I was just too startled to think straight.

'It's cancer.' She choked the word out in a strangled murmur, as though naming it was a step too far. 'Of the lungs.' As though to emphasise her words, they were followed by another one of her coughing fits.

'I don't understand. You're not that old . . . other than your cough, you seem fine. Can't they give you treatment?'

'It has spread too far – the only treatment they can give me now is to ease my pain. You know, at the end.'

'I can't believe that! There must be something they can do?'

'That's what I thought, at first.' She sighed. Seemed to shake herself. 'My precious darling, I haven't been entirely honest with you, I'm afraid. I've been going for hospital appointments for a while now.' She removed her turban, one of about ten she always wore on rotation.

Her hair was gone. I gasped.

'They already tried chemotherapy. It didn't work.'

I was furious with myself then. I'd been so wrapped up in Darsh. How could I not have noticed what my aunt was going through? Now I was looking at her properly, I could see her eyebrows were drawn on too. Her body looked thinner and frailer under her kaftan.

'Don't feel guilty, darling,' Wyn said, reading my mind. 'I'm a helluva actress when I put my mind to it. I didn't want you to know. I didn't want to spoil your time in London. Plus, it was nice not to think or talk about it for a bit. You know, during our evenings together.'

'But . . . You even carried on smoking!' I was angry with her now. For not telling me. For putting her health at risk with stupid fags. For making my heart break like it was breaking in that moment.

'It's an addiction, my darling. I tried to stop, but I couldn't. Even knowing the price I was paying. I'm sorry.'

I nodded, not trusting myself to answer her.

'Anyway, today was my last hope. A second opinion. The oncologist I saw today confirmed the prognosis of the first. I am . . . beyond cure.'

And with those words she began to sob. Huge, shoulder-shaking tears. I didn't know what I should do. It was so strange when people older than you cried. They were meant to comfort you, not the other way round.

Wyn made a strange sound halfway between a gulp and wail and it suddenly dawned on me how terrified she must be. I stood and walked around to her side of the table. I wrapped my arms around her. She rested her head on my forearm. I could feel the short fuzzy new hairs that had grown through since her old ones had fallen out. They were so soft, like a duckling's feathers. Her tears splashed against the skin of my arm.

We stayed like that for a while, not talking. In that moment we weren't a teenager and her guardian. We weren't even aunt and niece. We were just two sad, lost women who'd been keeping enormous secrets.

CHAPTER 30

She picked up after two rings.

'Hello?'

'It's me.'

'Well, this is a surprise! It's not even Sunday. I suppose you'll be wanting your da, will you?'

'No. It's you I'm wanting . . .' I began to cry.

'What's wrong, poppet?'

'I need your help.'

'I'm on my way.'

CHAPTER 31

Mam arrived the next morning, having taken the first train out of Camarthen. I had no idea where she was going to sleep that night. I suspected she didn't either. I hadn't thought it through; all I knew was that I needed her. It was so strange, after pushing her away and wanting to do things by myself for so long. After Wyn's confession, I'd felt a need for my mam which I couldn't ignore.

She took one look at me and literally dropped everything, her hastily packed bag thudding at her feet as she rushed towards me and swept me into a cwtch.

'There, there, now,' she soothed, stroking my hair. 'Nothing's insurmountable apart from death. Whatever it is, we'll work it out.'

She obviously didn't know about Wyn, or she wouldn't have said the thing about death. This didn't surprise me. Wyn would find the idea of Mam feeling sorry for her unbearable. Plus, it wasn't exactly a secret that they didn't get along. Wyn had even made herself scarce that morning. She made some sort of excuse about meeting a friend when I told her I'd invited Mam for a visit.

It was a cowardly move, leaving me to tell Mam the truth about her illness. That said, you couldn't exactly get angry with someone who had less than six months to live. If I was Wyn, I wouldn't relish spending the entirety of my remaining time on Earth telling people I was dying. Having to deal again and again with their shock, sadness and confusion.

'Let me make a cup of tea and then you can tell me what's wrong,' Mam said, sweeping into Wyn's kitchen and opening and closing all the cupboards. 'Where does Blodwyn keep her teapot?'

'Errr . . . I don't think she has one. We just make tea in cups,' I replied.

'Absolute savages in this London,' Mam muttered under her breath. Ordinarily I'd have been annoyed by this, but at that moment I was just so pleased to see her.

She made two cups of tea, sat at the table, took a sip of hers and made a big performance of wincing. For the second time in as many days, I took a seat in the other chair and prepared myself to have a big conversation.

'Wyn's not well,' I told her, spontaneously deciding to start with that and move on to my situation later.

'Oh, dear,' Mam said without much emotion. 'What is it? Got gout from drinking too many whisky sours again, has she?'

'No, Mam. It's more serious than that. It's cancer.'

Now it was my turn to say 'cancer', I realised why Wyn had found it so difficult. It was such an ugly word, with such enormous significance and power. It felt all wrong in my mouth.

Mam wanted to know how serious it was. When I told her Wyn's prognosis she buried her face in her hands.

'Why wouldn't she tell me?' Mam pondered. She seemed to be talking to herself, so I didn't reply.

'Mam,' I whispered, 'that's not the only thing. There's something else I need to tell you. I'm pregnant.' I got it out before I could stop myself. Then I let my words hang in the air between us, squinting slightly as I steeled myself for her reaction.

If you had asked me to guess how Mam would respond to the news that I was pregnant at the age of seventeen, I would have got it totally wrong. I'd have predicted that she would scream at me for being stupid. Perhaps for hours. Maybe talked about how she 'knew something like this would happen' the minute I'd announced that I was going to London. I wouldn't have put it past her to disown me.

In reality, she didn't say or do any of those things. Instead, she quietly said 'right' and then was silent for a few moments. I held my breath, ready for the explosion that never came. When she finally did speak, she was calm.

'And how do you feel about that?' she asked.

'I . . . have no idea,' I answered truthfully. 'Wyn told me her news just after I found out and it hasn't really sunk in. I guess . . . angry with myself? For being stupid?'

'Well, yes,' Mam replied wryly. 'Although it does take two to tango, as they say. Who is the father?'

I opened my mouth to respond then thought better of it. Darsh didn't even know yet. Not to mention Wyn, who would doubtless have an absolute shit fit.

'OK, you don't have to tell me right away if you don't want to. For now, let's talk about what you want to do. Do you want to keep the baby?'

'I don't know.'

'That's understandable. But there is a timeline on these thing, Cerys. If you don't decide for yourself soon then nature will make the decision for you. How many weeks gone are you?'

Then, quite suddenly, I wasn't angry with myself any more. I was raging at Mam. She was bombarding me with questions, smothering me within half an hour of walking through the door. Classic Mam style.

I stood up. 'I don't know, OK?' I bellowed at her. 'Stop asking me things I don't know!'

I turned to leave the kitchen, to stomp away like I always did when Mam annoyed me.

'I had an abortion once.'

Mam said it so quietly, at first I wasn't sure I'd heard her properly. I stopped in my tracks, turning to face her.

'What?'

'It was a long time ago. Fourteen years before you were even born.'

'Do you regret it?'

'In some ways. In others, not.'

'Does Da?'

'It wasn't his.'

I sat back down at the table and Mam kept talking. Every sentence she uttered destroyed another belief I had about myself and my family. My place in the world.

'I was married before I met your da. To a nasty bloke. He used to . . . knock me about.'

'I'm sorry, Mam.'

'Why should you be sorry? You didn't do it.'

'I'm sorry that happened to you.'

'Yes, well. It's more common than you think. At least I got out of it. But when he got me pregnant I knew I couldn't keep the baby. I couldn't bring a child into that house. I knew he would treat him or her just as badly as he had treated me. And I already knew I wanted to leave him. I didn't want to live my life with a constant reminder of that man. He was a monster. Do you understand?' Mam looked at me, pleading.

She'd never asked for my approval before. It was a weird sensation.

'Of course I understand,' I told her and she nodded, looking relieved. 'I managed to escape. Your nain and taid helped. And then I met your da and I knew straight away he was the one. I wanted to have a family with him. We tried for years but it never happened. I started to think the abortion had messed my insides up, you know? Dafydd said it didn't matter, that I was enough, but I knew he was secretly sad about it too. Then you came along and it was as though a miracle had happened.'

'But . . . but . . .' I stuttered. 'I always thought I was an inconvenience to you. That you'd rather not have had me.'

'Why on earth would you think that?'

'You're always cross with me.'

She sighed. 'I'm protective of you, Cerys – there's a difference. I don't like some of the choices you've made because they've put you in danger. Not because I'm trying to spoil your fun.'

I sat and absorbed this for a moment, taking all my memories and reshaping them with the benefit of this knowledge. As though my recollections were Play-Doh and Mam had just given me a new cookie cutter to push them through.

'You always seemed like you were trying to get away from me,' Mam said, after we'd sat in silence for a while, occasionally sipping tea just because it was there. 'Even when you were a little girl, other children would hold their mams' hands in the playground and you'd go running off before I'd even said goodbye.'

'I'm independent, Mam. There's nothing wrong with that. You could be proud.'

'I *am* proud of you, Cerys,' she said, which in some ways was the most shocking thing she'd told me. 'I'm just scared something will happen to you. You're my only child. You're precious to me.'

'Then why are you always shouting at me?'

'I'm not always shouting at you!' Mam shouted, then caught herself and laughed. In a more measured tone, she added, 'I can't pretend it's not hurtful, when you make it so obvious you prefer your da to me. And then there's how much you idolize Blodwyn.'

'I don't—' I began to protest, but she raised a hand to shut me up.

'There's no point in denying it. I've known you your whole

life, remember?' She smiled, then her faced dropped and she looked sad again. 'You're always pushing me away.'

'I'm sorry.'

Mam nodded.

'Well. I'm here now. We're going to face all this together. OK?'

I let myself breathe out. Everything I'd believed about my life so far might have been a lie, but at least Mam was here. She was like a lighthouse, drawing me back to the safety of the shore after I'd been out so long at sea.

CHAPTER 32

The walk from the Tube station to his flat felt too short. I dragged my feet, took pigeon steps; anything to avoid the moment where I'd have to say the words to him and change everything between us, for ever.

After buzzing me up, he opened the door to his flat and immediately turned and walked back inside without even glancing at me. He used to sweep me into his arms and then stare at me for a bit as soon as I crossed the threshold. As though he couldn't wait a millisecond longer to drink me in. I couldn't put my finger on exactly when or why it had changed.

I followed him into the living space and paced up and down in front of the French window, while he made tea. I'd rehearsed what I was going to say, like, three thousand times in front of the mirror in my bedroom. But now I was actually here, all the words I'd imagined saying seemed wrong. I was terrified. Not of him, exactly. But of doing or saying something that would make him retreat even further away from me.

You only ever get one chance to tell the love of your life that he'd got you up the duff and it was crucial I got it right. The responsibility was almost too much to bear.

He turned, expecting to see me sitting in my usual place on the sofa and looked startled to find me standing.

'What's wrong?'

'Nothing!' I replied reflexively, before realising that wasn't actually the case at all. 'I just need to talk to you about something.'

'OK.' He bent to place the two cups of tea he was holding on the coffee table and then came over to stand in front of me. 'What is it?'

'Darsh . . . Do you still love me?'

He looked relieved, as though he was worried I was going to ask him something less easy to answer.

'Of course! Why would you ever doubt that I did?'

'I feel like . . . things aren't the same between us.'

'Give me an example.'

'Like . . . You don't hug me at your front door any more. You just open the door and expect me to follow you inside.' It sounded a bit pathetic, now I'd said it out loud. I hoped he got what I meant.

He frowned, looking like he was deep in thought for a moment.

'No, I suppose I don't,' he replied, finally. 'We've been seeing each other for a long time now, Cerys. It's natural that the excitement fades a little. I'm more comfortable in your company now.' He hugged me to him and rested his chin on the top of my head, like he used to in the beginning. 'Sometimes I forget that you don't have experience of such things.'

I opened my mouth to object, to tell him that Rhys and

I were together for far longer and he still made me feel special right until the end. Well, up until the moment he called me a slag. Then I thought better of it.

I stayed silent for a while, enjoying the feeling of his embrace, the weight of his head on mine. I tried to commit every part of the moment to memory, knowing that if he took what I had to say badly I might never be here again.

I pushed my face into his T-shirt. I'd stay here until I ran out of breath. Then I'd tell him. 'Darsh?' I gasped, when I couldn't hold my breath any longer.

He chuckled. 'Yyyyessssss?'

'I have something else I need to tell you.'

He put his fingers under my chin and tilted my head up. It was excruciating, the way he was doing all the things he did when we first fell for each other. Just as I had a massive bombshell to drop.

'What is it, my love?'

I had to do it. I had to rip the plaster off. Like Mam said, if I didn't, nature would make the decision for me.

'I did a pregnancy test and it was positive,' I told him. Then I held my breath again as I awaited his reaction.

He stopped touching me and took a step back, almost stumbling on the corner of the coffee table as he did.

'How is that possible?'

'Come on, Darsh, you don't need me to explain how babies are made, do you?' I tried to laugh, hoping he'd join in. Everything would be all right if I could just made him smile.

'No, I . . . I thought you were using protection?'

'I was. It's not a hundred per cent effective.' He didn't respond. I carried on, just to fill the silence. 'Nothing is an absolute guarantee. There's always a risk–'

'HOW COULD YOU BE SO IRRESPONSIBLE?' he roared.

'Me? I didn't do this by myself, Darsh!' I said, gesturing at my stomach.

'You were the one who said not to use a condom! I wanted to! This is your fault!'

There was something new in how he was looking at me. It was as though he found me physically repulsive. I couldn't bear it. Everything had been OK twenty seconds ago.

'I'm sorry. I made a mistake. But I'm still the same person. I'm still the girl you love.'

He laughed. It was a horrible sound, with no warmth. 'Love you? My dear, if you think I ever really loved you you're even stupider than I realised.'

I felt my body go cold. I couldn't process the idea of him having those ideas in his head, let alone saying them out loud. 'You don't mean this, Darsh. You're just shocked.'

'Slutty British teenager gets herself pregnant. Nothing could be less shocking,' he spat.

I reeled, trying to make sense of this person in front of me. He looked like Darsh. He sounded like Darsh. But the things he was saying, my Darsh would never say. It couldn't be him. This must be a dream.

The Darsh who couldn't possibly be real continued to shout at me. 'I should never have gone near you! You dress like a slut and go out and get so drunk you can't remember what you did!

How do I even know this . . . situation . . . is anything to do with me?'

I was crying now, hot tears flowing freely down my cheeks. 'You know there's never been anyone else!' I pleaded.

'That's what you wanted me to believe. Now I know I was a fool to think I could trust you. You've been manipulating everyone around you since the day I met you. Why should I be the exception?'

He was right. That was the most painful thing. I couldn't even fight my corner because he'd seen who I really was. I'd deceived everyone in my life, including myself.

'Get out,' he said. His voice was quiet now. Menacing.

I did as he asked. I felt like I was in a trance as I got the lift to the ground floor, walked to the gates and pressed the button to make them open.

I walked until I was sure Darsh wouldn't be able to see me from his balcony. Then I found a bench to sink onto and I wept. I cried more loudly and messily than I ever had before.

So many thoughts were going through my head. I tried to tell myself that Darsh was just in shock. That, any second now, he'd send me a text saying he was sorry, he didn't mean what he said. Asking me to come back.

There was another, louder, voice inside me that wondered if today I'd just seen the real Darsh.

Again, my whole world tilted on its axis. What if I'd only fooled myself into believing I was happy with him? What if the whole time he had just been stringing me along, laughing at me?

I was such an idiot. The realisation descended on me like a heavy cloak. The thought was so claustrophobic, I was too weighed down with it to argue any more. There was nothing left to say.

Utterly defeated, I began to walk to the Tube. Further away from him. Away from all those months I'd spent thinking he loved me. Away from everything I thought I'd known.

CHAPTER 33

Mam was sleeping on a camp bed in Wyn's sitting room, lent to us by one of the neighbours. Wyn's place had never exactly been huge, but with three of us there it felt minuscule.

They bickered constantly. Mam thought the colour of Wyn's walls were 'oppressive'. Wyn countered that was because Mam had all the artistic leanings of a fruit fly.

Mam said the cost of milk and bread in the local shop was 'extortionate'. Wyn replied that it was a 'civilisation tax' – a cost worth it to be living away from 'provincial mundanity'.

Mam asked why Wyn didn't have dust ruffles on her beds. Wyn said, 'because it's not the 1950s and we aren't in a BBC comedy-drama.'

I knew Wyn probably thought our living scenario was less than ideal and I felt bad for causing her stress when she was so poorly. This couldn't go on indefinitely. Mam said she'd stay until I decided what I wanted to do and we could make a plan. The problem was, every time I thought I knew, I changed my mind.

The options looped around and around in my head – abortion/motherhood. Wales/London. College/not college.

I kept thinking that if I could definitely decide on one, the other two would become obvious.

If I wanted to carry on living in London and go to college, I had to have an abortion. If I wanted to keep the baby, I'd have to move back to Wales – which meant giving up college. And then what would I do with my life? Would my baby and I live for ever with Mam and Da? Did going through with this pregnancy mean I was signing up for a life I'd been plotting to escape from since the first time I'd seen a map and realised there were places other than Llangunnor? But then, it wasn't as though the life I had here was going so fabulously either.

My calls and texts to Darsh remained unanswered. Soon, Wyn would be gone. I couldn't be in London if I didn't have either of them to support me.

Did I still think London was where I needed to be? Did I want to carry on studying art? Did I want this baby? If only I could decide on just one of those things, then everything else would fall into place. Unfortunately for me, the answer to all three of those questions was 'kinda'.

Did I even believe abortion was right? If I convinced myself it was wrong, morally, that would actually be quite convenient. I wouldn't have to make a decision at all. It had already been made for me. There was a strange kind of comfort in that.

We'd had a debate about abortion at school, in English, once. The team who were against it brought in pictures of foetuses and told us when they started to feel and hear things.

I can't remember exactly when it was now, but I did recall that it was earlier than I'd expected. Then they asked us if we knew of a woman who already had five children and was living in poverty, if we'd support her aborting her sixth. Most of us said we would. Then they said what if we knew that sixth baby would have grown-up to be Martin Luther King, or Einstein? Shouldn't everyone have the chance to fulfil their destiny? Most of us changed our minds.

The team who were for abortion said women should have a choice. They said if a woman was raped, or she was in an abusive marriage, or going through the pregnancy would put her life in danger she shouldn't be forced to keep it. Most of us agreed with that too.

But I hadn't been raped. I wasn't in an abusive marriage. I wasn't in any sort of marriage at all. And I didn't know anything about the life growing inside me. Maybe it would be the next Einstein. But what if it was the next Hitler? None of examples we discussed seemed to apply, which made me wonder if I should even be considering abortion as an option.

I stayed in my bedroom for days, thinking and thinking until the thinking made me tired and then I slept. Then I'd wake up and think again. It was a strange, hermit-like existence. I kept my curtains closed, so I lost all track of when was day and when was night. The only time I left my room was to use the toilet. The rest of the time I lay on my bed thinking, while Mam brought me in cups of tea and sandwiches and reminded me she was here whenever I was ready to talk.

I heard Mam taking tea and sandwiches in to Wyn's room too. Wyn was also tired, for different reasons. I'd hear their low chatter, not being able to make out the words unless it descended into one of their squabbles. I'd briefly wonder what they were talking about, then get back to my thinking.

Then, one day, I woke up and realised I'd been wasting my time dwelling on the morality of abortion. No woman should be forced to have a baby she doesn't want, no matter the reason. Ultimately, I was thankful I had the right to choose.

It's just that having choice didn't make anything any easier for me.

So, then I was back to imagining the scenarios – college in London with the possible regret of aborting my baby? Or back where I started in Wales, with a baby?

The next time Mam came bustling in, pushing through the clothes curtain bum-first while holding a tray, it was different. She didn't just hand me my sandwich, pop a cuppa on the floor near my bed, remind me she existed and leave, like she had before. This time, she perched on the end of the bed and looked at me expectantly.

'I still don't know what I want to do, Mam. I'm sorry.'

'No need for sorries. You take all the time you need.'

'Thanks.'

We sat for a bit, not talking.

'I've noticed something,' Mam said, at last.

'What's that?' I asked, squinting.

'What's that face for?' Mam asked, half-laughing.

'I'm scared you're going to nag me about something.'

Mam playfully pinched my cheek and made a 'nnnggg' sound. Half-annoyed, half-affectionate. 'You don't listen to music any more.'

'I've been too busy thinking.'

'It's just a bit strange, that's all. Back home you were always blasting something out of that stereo of yours, or you'd have your headphones on. Don't you miss it?'

I thought about it. The truth was, it wasn't just while Mam had been there that I'd not been playing music. I couldn't remember the last time I'd put one of my CDs into my Walkman. I used to put songs on because they reflected the mood I was in. Or the one I wanted to be in. They helped me to escape, or focus.

I listened to pop, indie, rock, RnB. There was always something playing before . . . he came along.

Mam gave my hand a little squeeze. 'It was just a thought,' she said. 'I'll leave you be.'

As soon as she'd left the room I started scrabbling under the bed. I found my Walkman and the handful of CDs I'd brought with me, covered in dust. I put in my single of 'A Thousand Trees' by Stereophonics. I thought it might be a track loud enough to drown out my relentless, exhausting thoughts. I turned the volume up to max and braced myself for the impact of the noise. Nothing happened. The battery had died. I sighed.

Then I spotted the alarm clock on the bedside table. It was also a radio. I switched it on and turned the dial until it tuned into something interesting.

It was the beat that got me first. It energised me and I stood up for a reason other than to wee for the first time in days. Then I tuned into the lyrics and it felt like fate that had made me put the radio on in that moment.

The song faded and the DJ's voice came in.

'That was Destiny's Child with "Survivor".'

It wasn't so much that the lyrics directly related to where I was in that moment, or the decision I was trying to make. They just helped me believe in myself. Turns out, that was exactly what I needed.

I'd spent all these hours and days visualising what life would be like if I ventured down either fork of the road in front of me. I should have learnt by now – that was no way to make a choice. After all, I'd imagined a more glamorous version of myself prancing around London in Topshop vintage, surrounded by achingly cool friends. It had only served to disillusion and frustrate me when the reality hit.

Whatever I chose, I would never be able to predict how it would pan out. I had no idea what it would be like to be a woman who'd had an abortion. I had no idea what it would be like to give birth. Or to be someone's mam.

My brain would always make it better – or worse – than it would be in reality. So, it was probably time to tell my brain to shut up. This was something I'd have to decide on pure instinct. I'd trust my gut and then I'd trust myself to survive the consequences.

Later, I emerged from my pit. Mam and Wyn were sitting at the kitchen table, each clutching a mug. They both looked at me, identical expressions of expectation on their faces. It was the first time I'd ever thought that they looked alike.

'I know what I want to do,' I announced. 'I want to keep the baby.'

CHAPTER 34

Mam had given me a cwtch. Wyn just smiled. She looked too exhausted to get up from her chair.

'So, you both approve of my decision then?'

'It's not for us to approve or disapprove, love,' said Mam. 'We'd have supported you whatever you decided.'

'That's very reasonable of you,' I observed. 'How come you're being so reasonable?'

'I am an extremely reasonable person! Aren't I, Blodwyn?' Mam turned just in time to see Wyn pulling a face behind her back. 'Very funny, you two. Look, you had to arrive at your own conclusions. If you'd had felt railroaded in either direction you'd have ended up living your life full of regrets and that's not what I'd want for you.'

I nodded.

'So now we have to work out the practicalities of all this,' Mam said, dusting her hands.

'Yeah . . . I've been thinking about that too. I suppose I have to move back to Wales,' I said, sighing.

'Well, not necessarily,' Wyn interjected, then started to cough.

We waited for the fit to pass, Mam and I looking at each other, her mouth twisted with concern.

'Blodwyn and I have been talking,' Mam told me, as Wyn got her breath back.

'Delia,' Wyn interrupted. 'It is my dying wish for you not to call me by my full name. Wyn is fine. It is what everyone calls me, apart from you, and I suspect then only because you know it winds me up.'

'Fine. *Wyn* and I have been talking. We need to find out how far gone you are and when your due date is – but, whatever that turns out to be, it makes sense for you to finish off the year at college. There's only a couple of weeks left and it'd be a shame for all your hard work to be for nothing.'

I liked that idea. In fact, submitting my end-of-year project felt more important than it had ever been, in that moment.

'We then thought it probably made sense for you to come back home to Wales until the baby is born and probably for a little while afterwards. Wyn will need . . . specialist care by that stage so she wouldn't be here to keep an eye on you.'

'Right.'

'But,' Wyn took over then. 'After you're eighteen and whenever you feel ready to, I'd like you to move back here. If you want to, that is, darling.'

'But won't you . . . ?' I stopped myself. I couldn't finish the sentence.

'Yes, darling, I will indeed be dead by then. It's OK, you can say it. I have made my peace with it.' She looked sad for a moment, then seemed to shake herself out of it. My heart actually ached, watching her making such efforts to be brave. 'I own this' – she gestured at the walls of her flat – 'and I wish to . . . bequeath it to you.'

'I can't let you do that!' I gasped.

'Why not, darling? I don't have any children. No next of kin. You're the closest thing I have to a daughter. I was planning to leave my worldly goods to you, whenever I shuffled off this mortal coil. You're just getting them a little earlier than expected.'

'It makes sense,' Mam said gently. 'I know you don't want to be stuck in Llangunnor for ever. You'd have no rent or mortgage to pay, you'd just have to find money for food and bills for you and your little one. We can help you out. I can move in for a bit to help you. If you want me to, that is.'

'Won't Da mind?' I asked.

'Da is perfectly capable of looking after himself for a while,' Mam replied. 'And it won't do him any harm to miss me. As they say, absence makes the heart grow fonder.' I mimed being sick. Mam actually chuckled. 'He can visit too. We can work out all the finer details as we go. You have to admit though, love, it's a brilliant plan.'

'Cunning!' Wyn laughed. It was so good to see her smiling.

'OK!' I grinned back. I was suddenly excited. The future was shaping up to be something I could be enthusiastic about. Perhaps.

'Now, I don't want to nag,' Mam said, at which Wyn and I both raised our eyebrows at her.

'Darling, nagging is your primary hobby. It is your number one skill. It is your raison d'être!' Wyn joked.

'Some of us have a sense of responsibility!' Mam rounded on Wyn.

'May I remind you that I am a dying woman?' Wyn opened her eyes wide and clutched her hands to her chest.

Mam raised her eyes to the ceiling. 'You are only allowed to use that to shirk duties or avoid arguments a maximum of twice per day. It's already getting tiresome.'

'Oh, SORRY if my incurable cancer inconveniences you, darling,' Wyn pouted.

I had to laugh. It was like they'd regressed to being children again.

'You two! Give it a rest!' I wagged my finger at them, enjoying the role-reversal. 'What do you not want to nag me about, Mam?'

'The father.'

'Oh.' I glanced at Wyn, wondering how she'd react if I revealed his identity. If she'd already guessed. If she'd told Mam.

'You have to tell him.'

'I already did. He made it . . . very clear that he doesn't want anything to do with me.'

'Does he know you are planning to keep the baby?'

'No. I hadn't even decided myself the last time I saw him.'

'Whoever he is, he deserves to know.'

Last time I'd seen Darsh it was like he'd put my heart in a blender and reduced it to mush. Just the thought of seeing him again was enough to make me shake. But, I realised with a sinking feeling, Mam was right.

CHAPTER 35

'I can't do this. I can't. I just cannot'.

I couldn't believe I was standing outside Darsh's block of flats again, ready to have another confrontation.

'Of course you can,' said Alice breezily. 'You are brave and feisty and awesome and you're going to be someone's mum.'

Once again, I found myself so grateful for her presence. I didn't want to go back to Darsh's alone, but Wyn was too frail and I couldn't guarantee Mam wouldn't try and wrestle him to the ground and tear chunks of his flesh out with her teeth in revenge for hurting me. That was, I was realising, what parenthood was about. Behaving in ways that were totally mad to protect your child.

'You're right, I need to do it for my baby,' I replied, a sudden wave of maternal instinct sweeping over me.

Alice put her hands on my shoulders. 'Do it for you. You deserve – what do they call it in American TV shows? Oh yeah, "closure". You need closure on this thing.'

The previous day, I'd gone to find Alice at the café. I needed my proxy big sister.

She'd locked up the café and took me to her halls of residence.

It was two bus rides away and smelt strongly of a combination of old pizza and weed. Once we were in her room, she put a CD in her player and went to make us hot chocolate.

'Make yourself at home,' she said.

I sat on a beanbag and looked at the posters on Alice's walls. One was the cover of a book – *The Passion of New Eve* by Angela Carter. It showed a black and white image of a woman wearing dark lipstick, crawling through a curtain with sparks coming out of her head.

Next to it was a poster of two women in white vests and jeans.

When Alice came back in holding two steaming mugs I pointed to the picture of the women and asked, 'Who are they?'

'A band called t.A.T.u. They're Russian. It's a total cliché for lesbians to like their stuff but they're talented and fit, so, what can you do?' she shrugged and laughed.

'Is that who we're listening to now?' I asked.

'No, actually. This is Meredith Brooks. Like it?'

'Yeah! What's this song called?'

'It's called 'Bitch'. It's about letting women be different things.'

'How do you mean?'

'Well, like, as a society' – Alice folded herself onto her bed and sat cross-legged, all the while managing not to spill her hot chocolate – 'we tend to divide women into categories. Some get to be "nice girls" and others are labelled as sluts or whores. That's just one example. But the point this song is making is that we all have the capacity for niceness and most of us are slutty sometimes. Or, you know, into sex, which there shouldn't actually be any judgment around.'

It was so on the nose that I had to say something.

'My ex' – it was too painful to say his name out loud – 'called me slutty when we broke up.'

'Classic.' Alice tutted. 'They need to hate you to justify breaking up with you and avoid examining their own behaviour. The only way they could do that was by reducing you to a stereotype.'

I nodded. 'Do you think it's built in. Like, a caveman thing? Being so obsessed with virginity and stuff?' I asked, dimly remembering a psychologist arguing that point in a magazine I read once.

'No. In fact, there are tribes where everyone shags everyone else and no one knows whose babies are whose and they all just chip in with the childcare.'

'Sounds great.' I laughed.

'It's patriarchy,' Alice said. 'That's the reason women are put into these arbitrary categories and punished accordingly. It's a way of dehumanising us. Like Meredith Brooks is saying in these lyrics – humans are complicated. We're all loads of different things and that doesn't necessarily make us good or bad. But only men get to be seen as three-dimensional.'

'I'm about to become the stereotype of the teenage mum,' I said, thinking this was as good a way of breaking it to Alice that I was pregnant as any. 'Do you think people will be able to see beyond that?'

I saw her absorb my news and, just like I knew she would, decide not to make a big deal out of it. 'The people who matter will know you're still you. Others will make assumptions.

But fuck them, frankly. It's your life. What did your auntie say?'

'She's been great. Really supportive. But she has her own stuff going on. She's not very well.'

'I'm sorry to hear that,' Alice responded.

'She has . . . cancer.' God, why was that word so hard to say out loud? 'It's terminal.'

Alice didn't say anything for a moment, just looked down at her mug. 'That's what Aimee died of.'

'Oh god. I'm so sorry. I didn't mean to bring back bad memories.'

'Don't be daft. I actually like to be reminded of her. Not the part where she was ill, obviously. But after someone dies young, people are scared to mention them and it ends up feeling like they never existed at all . . .'

'What was she like – Aimee?' I asked.

'She was really funny. When I remember her, she is always laughing. But she was also really brave. She would say if she didn't think something was fair. I remember her standing up in front of the whole school in assembly once and objecting when a guest speaker started talking about homosexuality being sinful. I'd just come out to Mum and Dad. I didn't have the bottle to say anything. But she did.'

'She sounds awesome.'

'She really was. Like I said, there's something about you that reminds me of her. I think it's because you're both free spirits.'

We sipped our hot chocolates for a bit, not talking, not feeling the need to.

'If you need help with anything. You know . . . while your auntie is dealing with all of this, just ask. I know how hard it all is,' Alice said, leaning over to rub my arm.

'There is something,' I replied. 'Something I need help with. It's not really related to Wyn, though. Sorry.'

'You don't have to apologise, Cerys. We're friends. It's what friends do.'

And that was how Alice ended up coming with me to tell Darsh that he was going to be a father. I was about to press the buzzer for his flat when a car came through the front gates. I slipped in, gesturing for Alice to follow me. Something told me it was better to surprise him at his front door. If he was forewarned, he might not buzz me up. We hadn't exactly parted on friendly terms.

Alice and I took the lift in silence. I was too nervous to say anything. Alice grabbed my hand and gave it a little squeeze.

'Do you want me to come in with you or wait here?' Alice asked, when we reached the sixth floor and the doors pinged open.

'Maybe hang around here if that's OK, and then I'll call you if I need you,' I replied nervously. I didn't want to admit it, but I wanted Alice within calling distance. I'd seen a totally different side to Darsh and I wasn't sure what that version of him was capable of.

The door to Darsh's flat was ajar. Still, I knocked on it, stopping short of striding into his place unannounced. There was no reply.

'Darsh?'

My voice echoed. Something wasn't right, I could sense it. I pushed the door with one finger. It swung open. I stepped inside.

'Darsh?' I tried again. 'It's Cerys. I need to talk to you. Hello?' I was tiptoeing, for some reason I couldn't explain.

Darsh's flat had never exactly been rammed with personal objects, but even the few bits he did have – the heavy black pan he used to make rice in, his shampoos and soaps in the bathroom, the art books on the bedside cabinet – weren't there.

After going into every room and finding it empty, I finally understood. Darsh was gone. He had simply disappeared.

It was like he never existed at all.

CHAPTER 36

Alice walked me all the way back to my front door. We didn't agree that was what she would do. In fact, we hardly talked on the journey.

When we got to Wyn's flat she asked, 'You'll be OK?'

I gulped and blinked back tears. I'd cried so much during the past few weeks I was surprised I had any left. Alice hugged me. We stayed like that for a while, the door open, until we heard Mam say, 'Who's letting the warm air out? Cerys . . . Oh! Hello!'

'Mam, this is my friend Alice.'

'Nice to meet you, Mrs Williams,' Alice said politely.

'And you, Alice. Call me Delia, please. You'll have a cup of tea.' It wasn't a question.

Alice and Wyn sat at the table, I perched on the windowsill and Mam did the hostess thing she was so good at.

Wyn had scrambled to put on her turban when she saw Alice walk into the room. Alice had waited until it was on before introducing herself. It broke my heart a bit, that Wyn thought she had to do that.

'I went to see the father today,' I said, once tea had been

distributed and a plate of neatly arranged biscuits placed on the table.

'And?' Mam and Wyn said in perfect unison.

'He wasn't there.'

'Couldn't you have waited for him?' asked Mam.

'Be good to get it over with I imagine, darling,' Wyn agreed.

'It's not like that. His door was open. His things were gone . . . *He's* gone, I think.'

'Run away, looks like,' Alice confirmed.

'The absolute and total shitbag,' replied Wyn.

'Agreed. Complete shitbag,' echoed Mam, which surprised me. She hardly ever swore.

'Is it that Darsh fellow?' asked Wyn. I nodded and I saw her and Mam exchange a glance.

I sensed that Wyn had already told Mam about Darsh. That that was one of the things they must have been whispering about while I was holed up in my room, making my Big Choice. It occurred to me that it must have been when they hatched the plan for me to return to London with the baby, too.

Mam and Wyn were a brilliant double act, when they weren't squabbling. They probably even loved each other, though a lot of time it seemed like hate. Maybe that was how all siblings were.

Wyn drew breath to add something else but then started to cough. Mam took over.

'Does this affect your decision? You know . . . about the baby?'

'No. I think I always knew I'd be doing it alone.'

'You're not alone,' said Wyn, having got her breath back. 'You have me.'

'And me,' said Mam.

'And me,' said Alice.

I looked at the three of them and felt as though my heart would burst.

I registered with a doctor and booked an appointment, which confirmed that I was due in late March 2002. That meant my baby would either be a Pisces, like me – romantic, sensitive, arty – or Aries, who were meant to be determined, confident and fiery. I kind of hoped it was the latter. I didn't want my baby to have their heart broken the way mine had been. I wanted a child who wouldn't stand for any crap from the Darshes or Rhyses or Sophias or Spencers they encountered in their lives.

The following week, Mam went back to Wales. She seemed reluctant about it and made me promise to tell her if I or Wyn needed her at any time. In the meantime, she'd call every day to check in.

I tried to be as normal as I could around Wyn, knowing she would hate it if she thought I was adjusting my behaviour or saw her differently just because she was sick. Dying. But it was hard. It was as though I could actually see her spirit being sucked out of her. Her skin was sallow, her face looked gaunt, her voice was getting quieter. Every morning I was shocked by how much smaller she seemed than the day before.

I started to get pregnancy sickness and at one point we

seemed to be spending most of the day taking it in turns to go to the bathroom to throw up.

Wyn decided Mooch should live with Tom and his husband. Watching the cat's sad, confused face through the window of his plastic carrycase as Tom took him to the car, I actually ached. There was no way to explain to Mooch that it wasn't that his Mam didn't love him, she was just too weak to look after him properly. That she would soon be gone. We just had to hope that he somehow knew through a kind of animal sixth sense. The flat immediately felt different without him.

Twice a day, carers visited to check on Wyn. They'd take her blood pressure, ask if she was in pain, make sure she was taking her medication. Wyn would put on a show for them, laughing and saying, 'it's terribly flattering to have all this attention, darlings.' I knew at some stage the carers wouldn't be enough and Wyn would have to go into a hospice, but no one could predict exactly when that would be. It felt like we were playing a surreal waiting game, with the highest stakes imaginable.

Wyn slept a lot and while awake was mostly getting her affairs in order. Death certainly did seem to involve a lot of admin. When she wasn't in bed or talking to solicitors, she asked me about college. Sometimes, when I answered her questions, she'd close her eyes. 'Carry on, darling. I'm listening, just resting my eyelids,' she'd say.

I told her about my final project. The kitchen, where I'd go to work on it after college, was mostly taken up with it now. Wyn wasn't eating much anyway and didn't seem to mind.

'I think it's genius,' she said, smiling, keeping her eyes closed. 'I'm very proud of you, I hope you know that.'

I swallowed, trying not to cry in front of her. 'I know.'

On the day when we were to display our final pieces, we set them up in the morning in the college hall. It was the very same place that demeaning picture of me had been projected, all those months ago, which seemed fitting. In the afternoon, we were allowed to return to see everyone's work, like it was an art gallery.

We were also allowed to invite family members to the unveiling. Wyn couldn't really leave the house and it was too far for Mam and Da to come, so I'd asked Alice. I couldn't have done it without her, after all. I figured we could say we were sisters, if asked. It wasn't like anyone was going to check.

Alice and I walked around in a slow circle, looking at what everyone had created. There were photographs and paintings, installations and mixed media pieces. The only rule was we had to showcase what we had learnt that year.

Alice was satisfyingly scathing about Sophia's work, which was a black and white self-portrait. I could tell she was trying to look as though she was wearing no make-up. Her hair was poker straight and centre parted and she was in plain black skinny jeans and a white T-shirt, barefoot, sitting on a backwards chair with her chin resting on one fist. The whole thing was very obviously an attempt to mimic Kate Moss. I couldn't deny that it was pretty, but I didn't really understand what she was trying to say with it.

'Total fucking derivative bollocks,' was Alice's assessment.

Eventually, we got to mine. Alice didn't say anything for a long time. She just stood and stared. I was worried she was thinking that my work was derivative bollocks too, but then she finally spoke.

'It's incredible, Cerys.'

'You actually have to put the headphones on and press play to get the full experience,' I told her. She did as instructed and I could just about make out the tinny sound of 'Bitch' by Meredith Brooks. The song we'd listened to in her room.

I looked at my piece again, trying to work out what it looked like through Alice's eyes.

Like Sophia's, it was a self-portrait. Unlike hers, I wasn't trying to look pretty, put-together or small. Quite the opposite, in fact.

I'd recreated my position in the projected photo. I was sprawled on the pavement at the bottom of Spencer's stairs. One leg was bent at a right angle, my skirt hitched up, my knickers on show. My handbag was to the right of me, some of the contents spilling out. Instead of my eyes being half-closed, like they were in the original image, I was looking directly into the camera. I was daring the viewer to judge me.

On the brick wall behind me, I'd added graffiti. The words 'slut' and 'slag' were scrawled in large, angry red writing. There was also the word 'daughter'. Next to that I'd glued a Polaroid of Mam and Da standing outside the farmhouse with Gruff. 'Niece' was written by an old snap of me as a child, sat cross-legged on the carpet at the farmhouse, looking enraptured as Wyn spun a yarn from the armchair.

'Friend' appeared alongside a recent photo of Alice and I, behind the counter at Sunny Side, in our ridiculous aprons.

On my stomach I'd written the word 'mother'. On my chest I'd painted a delicate, pink and white lotus flower. My mouth was overlaid with the green, red and white of the Welsh flag, as though it was lipstick.

My Walkman was one of the items that had spilt out of my handbag. Around it, I'd glued images of my favourite artists cut from the covers of their CDs. There were the Manics, and I'd written the title line from their song 'If You Tolerate This Your Children Will Be Next' underneath. There were the Stereophonics, alongside a few lyrics from 'A Thousand Trees', about how quickly gossip spreads. There was Destiny's Child next to the word 'Survivor'.

Also rolling out of my bag was a glittery eyeshadow duo, a folded paper map of the London Underground and a packet of custard creams.

The text below the image read:

> This is a picture of someone's daughter. Of a woman about to become someone's mother. A person who had her heart broken by a charismatic man who gave her a lotus flower. Who speaks with a Welsh accent and has found herself in a strange new city. Who loves music and sparkly make-up. Who, if she was a biscuit, would be a custard cream. A person with layers. A woman who decided to reclaim the humiliation that has been forced upon her and change the story. This is me. My name is Cerys Williams.

This wasn't just a picture of a silly girl who got too pissed to stand and was snapped with her knickers on show. This wasn't just some object to be laughed at.

Around the picture of me I'd glued hundreds more pictures from magazines of women who'd also been humiliated by the camera's lens. Women with rings drawn around their 'flaws'. Women snapped halfway through eating a sandwich. Women whose underwear, or upper thighs, or nipples could be seen. Women who looked like they might have had a drink.

This was the culture I'd grown-up in. These photos were everywhere, the water we were all swimming in. We'd learnt the response was to disapprove and feel superior, without thinking about who these people really were. Because we weren't supposed to believe we were like the women in these photos. We'd never be so stupid or careless as to stumble about drunk with our pants – or cellulite – on display.

Yet every one of those women was someone's daughter. Some of them were someone's mum. Every one of them had hopes and dreams and fears and passions. They probably could be a bitch, but could also be kind. Every one of them had exes, some of them probably had broken hearts. All of them had friends.

As I looked at Alice, it occurred to me that she could easily be part of the installation. She was standing at about the same distance as when she'd taken the photo. She had helped me to remember who the woman in it was. Who I was.

I felt a tap on my shoulder and turned to see Kate standing just behind me. Her eyes were shining.

'Your best work yet,' she said.

'Thank you. I couldn't have done it without you,' I replied.

'It was my pleasure. I'm really proud of what you've achieved.'

In that moment, I was proud of myself too.

We were interrupted by a familiar clip-clopping sound of shoes on hard floor.

'Ms Williams.' It was the principal.

'Hi,' I responded, warily.

'I understand that, owing to your . . . erm . . . circumstances' – he glanced pointedly at my belly – 'you will be leaving us at the end of this term.'

'That's right,' I replied.

'I want you to know that, if you do decide to return to complete your second year, you will be very welcome. This piece' – he gestured to my work – 'is extraordinary. It would be our honour to continue to nurture your very obvious talent as an artist.'

'Wow.' I was stunned.

'Congratulations.' He patted my shoulder, glanced at my stomach again and wandered away.

'I hope you do come back,' added Kate, still looking at my piece. 'I'm looking forward to seeing what you do next'.

CHAPTER 37

Wyn went into a hospice in the middle of October. I'd been for a scan a couple of weeks earlier, which had confirmed my baby girl was healthy. Mam came to stay with me in Wyn's flat. We knew she didn't have long. We visited her daily. Sometimes we'd bump into her friends, also visiting. Tom and his husband, with updates on Mooch (who was apparently having 'terrific fun' chasing the mice that occasionally found their way into his new home). The famous Organza, who painted Wyn's nails in gorgeous ombre shades of orange and purple. The man from the Lebanese restaurant Wyn had taken me to when I first arrived in London, who turned out to be called Khalil.

When we weren't visiting, we cleared Wyn's cupboards and sorted her things. Worked out what should be kept and what could be thrown away. It was as much something to do as anything, while we waited for the inevitable phone call telling us it was time.

During one of our visits, Mam had gone to get some fresh air, leaving Wyn and I alone. Wyn was in her usual spot, lying in her bed surrounded by machines that bleeped, a clear plastic mask in her hand for when she needed more oxygen.

Her voice was now barely more than a whisper and she had to take huge, heaving breaths between words. It was devastating to see the painful decline of a woman who had always been so full of life. This wasn't Wyn. Wyn was loud, colourful, just a little bit too much.

'I suppose I ought to impart some wisdom to you before I go,' Wyn gasped.

'It's OK,' I reassured her, not wanting her to strain herself. 'Nain already told me the Evans family motto when she . . . I mean, when I was thirteen.'

'What did she tell you?' Wyn asked.

'She said life is about the little decisions, not the big ones. That turning down a certain street or spontaneously deciding to get a bun from the bakers can change the whole course of your life. That's why I moved to London. More streets to turn into. Well, and to be with you of course.' I squeezed her hand gently.

'Interesting,' Wyn muttered, looking out the window for a while. 'I think, though, the streets are more of a symbolic thing.'

I thought about how many symbolic streets I'd turned down in the past year, that had altered the course of my life. The spontaneous decision – that had felt like an instinct – to disturb Darsh as he sat outside Sunny Side that day. Kissing him at Diwali. Saying 'yes' when Sophia asked me to Spencer's house party, even as my gut warned against it. Not being as careful as I should have been to take my pill at the same time every day. Prioritising his fun and saying no to a condom. Randomly switching on the radio and listening to a song with lyrics that made me believe I had the power to decide. That I could be happy whichever choice I made.

'I do love you, Cerys, you know,' Wyn cut into my thoughts. I tried to squeeze my throat shut. I knew she would want to say goodbye. I just didn't know if I was strong enough to hear it.

'I know. I love you too,' I said, my voice squeaking as I tried to stop my tears.

'You are my legacy, darling. Speaking of which, I have a secret to tell you.' She beckoned me and I ducked my head, bringing my ear to her lips.

'You're not just getting the flat. You'll get everything. My savings. Life insurance. Everything left after legal and funeral expenses is left to you. There's enough for you to make a start for yourself and your little one in London. Whenever you're ready.'

I was stunned. 'I don't know what to say.'

'Delia thinks I'm irresponsible, but I was saving for a retirement in the South of France,' she rasped. 'No use to me now.'

I nodded, knowing there were no words that would be good enough. Nothing I could say to tell her how grateful I was, how much this meant. How futile it would be to say what I was really feeling, which was that I wished I wasn't being given these life-changing riches. I'd much rather she could spend it all on her French retirement.

'I don't want you to go,' I suddenly blurted out, childishly, as though she had any say in the matter.

'I know.'

She patted my hair weakly as I laid my head on her stomach and allowed my tears to flow until her blanket was soaked.

If I thought Darsh had broken my heart, it was nothing to what I was feeling now. This was pain so raw it was like my whole body was being torn in two.

'Sorry,' I hiccupped, when I'd cried out all the moisture in my body.

'Don't be sorry. It'd be worse if you didn't care, darling.'

'It's just so unfair.'

'Death is inevitable,' Wyn replied. She drew a circle with the finger of one hand. 'Circle of life. As one leaves, another enters . . .' She pointed at my tummy.

'I was thinking, I will call her Blodwyn – after you,' I said.

'Absolutely not,' said Wyn.

'Why?'

'Well, first of all, I hate my name. And secondly, it means "white flower" in Welsh. And she is going to be . . .'

'Not white. Yes, OK. Good point,' I said.

Wyn yawned. I knew she'd be asleep soon, and every time she nodded off there was a chance she wouldn't wake up.

'OK, well, what's a better name . . . ? I want her to be strong. Not scared to make her voice heard. Able to stand up for herself. I want her to kick ass, if I'm honest.'

Wyn made a noise too quiet for me to hear.

'What was that?' I bent down again.

'You should call her Llewella,' Wyn said. 'It means "brave".'

CHAPTER 38

New Message

From: D_Nadeem@yahoo.com

To: Cerys.Williams@TheHiddenArtGallery.co.uk

21:14 Feb 20, 2012

Dear Cerys,

I hope you are well. I was able to obtain your email address from the principal at your old college in Chelsea. He told me you continue to be an inspiration to current students because of all you have achieved since graduating. Congratulations.

He also confirmed what I already suspected. Your daughter is almost ten. I had managed to convince myself she did not exist. I believed if I cut off contact with you it would force you to terminate the pregnancy. I did not think you would want to raise the child with no partner to support you. I underestimated you and I am ashamed of that now.

Please know that I did love you, sincerely and deeply. However, I was not entirely honest with you.

When I came to London, I was already engaged. My parents had granted me a year away, at their expense, to explore whichever part of the world I chose before settling down. I did not expect to meet someone for whom I had such strong feelings. At first, I thought perhaps there might be a way for us to be together. I wondered if I might be able to talk my parents around and take you home with me. As our relationship progressed, I realised our cultural differences were too significant for us to surmount.

I know I owe you more of an explanation and I hope you will be gracious enough to meet with me so I can provide you with it. I will be in London for the next three months before I return home again. I would very much like the opportunity to meet your daughter, too, while I am here. I am now married with two children of my own, so this matter would have to remain highly confidential.

Although the one we spent together was not romantic in the traditional sense, every Valentine's Day I find myself thinking of you.

Please write to me at the above address if you would consent to a meeting. I remain hopeful.

Yours,
Darsh

EPILOGUE
8 years later

I insisted on driving Llewella to school to pick up her A level results, even though it was less than a mile away. It seemed like the right thing for the significance of the occasion.

I could tell she was nervous. I glanced across to the passenger seat and saw her twisting her hands in her lap, looking out of the window. I'd told her I'd be proud of her whatever she got, but she was her own harshest critic. She set such high standards for herself.

I looked over at her again, her wavy dark hair shining in the sunlight and struggled to contain myself. I could never have imagined I'd produce such a brilliant daughter. My only wish for her was that she would be brave, and so she had turned out – but she was also thoughtful, creative, clever, articulate and a million other things. Too many to name.

I was working very hard on not allowing myself to become overwhelmed and emotional, knowing Loo needed me to be calm. No one prepares you for how much you will love your children. No one tells you how it feels because it's indescribable. You're consumed with it. Every time they're hurt, or sad, or wronged, you feel as though it's happening to you. You want to protect them from it, but you also know there are some lessons they have to learn for themselves.

So much of how my mam was with me makes sense, now. Still, I'd done my best to be different, to give Loo space and freedom so she'd never resent me, or do something silly because she felt trapped.

That's why I'd forced myself to watch without interfering over the past year, as my daughter tried on a new identity. One that really didn't suit her. It was so frustrating, to witness someone you love make mistakes. Yet I knew I had to let her make them.

After all, as much as I respected her, there was nothing Wyn could have said which would have stopped me falling for Loo's father. My love for him was a kind of madness. He was so mysterious, only giving me little glimpses of who he was. I filled in all the blanks with who I wanted him to be. I created and fell for a fantasy. It's so easy to do, when you're vulnerable and they're charming.

I watched Loo climb the stone stairs which led up to the entrance of St Edith's and saw her friend – or, I suppose that should be, former friend – Aretha emerge. The two of them faced off. I held my breath, wondering whether there'd be a confrontation. I was too far away to make out any of what they were saying, but Aretha seemed to shrink a little, as though she was ashamed. I recognised in my daughter's body language that she'd decided to be kind. To let her go. To let it go, perhaps. Good decision, if so.

I was pretty sure Loo's infatuation with Aretha had been

platonic. Although that didn't make it any less powerful. It had still messed with her head and changed her behaviour. Still diminished her whilst she was in its clutches.

From what I can piece together from the small glimpses of their friendship I've seen (including the YouTube videos from Loo's vlog that she doesn't know I watch) it seems as though Aretha tried to shrink Loo on purpose. With Darsh, he was careless with my heart but I don't think he was ever malicious like that. He hurt me because he was self-absorbed, scared and far more immature than his demeanour would suggest. That's why I never replied to his email, the one he sent when Loo was almost ten. It was clear from what he wrote that he hadn't changed.

Aretha was something else entirely. Some teenage girls find such elaborate and subtle ways to torture each other and undermine one another's self-esteem. Like Sophia did to me. God, her behaviour had left me with scars. Or a babushka, as that Valentina would have said.

But then there are the girls that restore your faith in humanity. Like Olivia, who I could see tripping up the steps of the school to meet Loo now, all colourful clothes and lack of co-ordination. She was so kind. A true friend, with Llewella's best interests at heart. She was a lot like Alice, now I thought about it.

I wondered what Alice was doing now. In the final year of her degree she fell in love with an Australian zoologist and relocated to be with her after graduating. I should try and look her up on Facebook. It would be nice to reminisce about those first few years of Loo's life, when we lived in Wyn's place in Ealing together. They say friends come into your life for a reason or a season. I can't imagine how I would have got through that season of my life if Alice hadn't been there.

Loo and Olivia linked arms, using their free hands to push open the door to the school. This was it. In the next few minutes they'd be collecting their envelopes. The ones containing the four little letters that would decide the next part of their future. They're such arbitrary things, exam results. They measure so little but determine so much.

And yet, as I watched my daughter disappear into the building to learn her fate, I knew, whatever those envelopes contained, she was going to be OK.

Acknowledgments

Thank you to my agent, Anna Pallai, who apart from getting the deal for this book, continues to be the calmest, most patient, least-inclined-to-blow-smoke-up-my-bum person in the world.

Thank you, Hazel Holmes and the team at UCLan for publishing this and letting me get Cerys's story out there. Thank you also Hazel for suggesting I binge-watch *Ginny & Georgia* during the writing process. It didn't really influence the book in the end but I had a fantastic time watching it and justified it as 'working'.

Thank you to my editor, Emma Roberts. I remain totally bowled over by your ability to look at a manuscript and know exactly what it needs. It's like a magical power. This book would be much less EVERYTHING without your input.

Finally, thank you to my Uncle Andy, who is a fine artist and offered me insights on Cerys's journey to becoming one herself (i.e. replied with lengthy and thoughtful offerings when I texted him saying 'is this something an arty person would think or is it total bollocks?').

I can't believe the last word of this book is 'bollocks'.

About the Author

Photo by Jonathan Donovan.

Natasha Devon MBE is an activist, writer and presenter. She tours schools, universities and events throughout the world, delivering talks as well as conducting research on mental health, body image, gender & equality. She has a show on LBC and writes regularly for *Grazia* Magazine.

Natasha is a trustee for the charity Student Minds, an ambassador for the Reading Agency and a patron for No Panic, which helps people experiencing anxiety. She is also an ambassador for Glitch; a charity which promotes digital citizenship, helping marginalised communities stay emotionally safe online. She is a certified instructor for Mental Health First Aid England and eating disorder charity, Beat.

In 2018, Natasha co-founded 'Where's Your Head At', a campaign aimed at improving the mental health of British workers through education and law change. She is also founder of the Mental Health Media Charter, which scrutinises media reporting on mental health with the aim of reducing stigma.

Her book *A Beginner's Guide to Being Mental: An A-Z* was published by Bluebird in 2018, followed by *Yes You Can: Ace Your Exams Without Losing Your Mind* in 2020. This is Natasha's second novel.

Find out more at www.natashadevon.com

IF YOU LIKE THIS, YOU'LL LOVE . . .

Student ID
19801219
Name:
ANNA C
Valid u
30 July
The Nicest Girl
Set boundaries.
Be honest.
Say no.
SOPHIE JO

HAVE YOU EVER WONDERED HOW BOOKS ARE MADE?

UCLan Publishing is an award winning independent publisher specialising in Children's and Young Adult books. Based at The University of Central Lancashire, this Preston-based publisher teaches MA Publishing students how to become industry professionals using the content and resources from its business; students are included at every stage of the publishing process and credited for the work that they contribute.

The business doesn't just help publishing students though. UCLan Publishing has supported the employability and real-life work skills for the University's Illustration, Acting, Translation, Animation, Photography, Film & TV students and many more. This is the beauty of books and stories; they fuel many other creative industries! The MA Publishing students are able to get involved from day one with the business and they acquire a behind the scenes experience of what it is like to work for a such a reputable independent.

The MA course was awarded a Times Higher Award (2018) for Innovation in the Arts and the business, UCLan Publishing, was awarded Best Newcomer at the Independent Publishing Guild (2019) for the ethos of teaching publishing using a com*merci*al publishing house. As the business continues to grow, so too does the student experience upon entering this dynamic Masters course.